ON CALL

l   ng, the slender, studious registrar
a   e Central London Hospital, had a
b   nt career ahead of him. He was on his
v   he top – and Sophie, the girl he
l   s by his side. Then, out of the blue,
l   like Louise arrived from Spain –
a   ck's life began to disintegrate. Tragic,
s   eemingly friendless, Louise clung
t   e a limpet. She brought Nick
n   trouble. He lost his job at the
C   e lost the flat where he and Sophie
h   d to live – and it began to look as if
h w   e Sophie too...

ON CALL

On Call

by

Elizabeth Harrison

Dales Large Print Books
Long Preston, North Yorkshire,
BD23 4ND, England.

British Library Cataloguing in Publication Data.

Harrison, Elizabeth
     On call.

          A catalogue record of this book is
          available from the British Library

          ISBN   978-1-84262-730-3 pbk

First published in Great Britain by Hurst & Blackett Ltd.

Cover illustration © Mohamad Itani by arrangement with
Arcangel Images

The moral right of the author has been asserted

Published in Large Print 2009 by arrangement with
Watson, Little Ltd.

Dales Large Print is an imprint of Library Magna Books Ltd.

Printed and bound in Great Britain by
T.J. (International) Ltd., Cornwall, PL28 8RW

CONTENTS

CHAPTER ONE

SURGICAL REGISTRAR
AT THE CENTRAL

Round about ten o'clock that night, Nick Waring and Sophie Field were sitting on the big chesterfield in front of the fire, drinking coffee and planning their future together.

The high-ceilinged room had the perfect proportions of Georgian architecture, and made a spacious background for the furniture from Nick's old home – Matthew Waring's roll-top desk, a sturdy chest of drawers, and the gate-legged table. There was a Welsh dresser, too, housing his surgical textbooks and journals, the microscope he'd had as a student. The flat, Sophie thought, was like Nick himself. Quiet and studious. Tall, slight, dark-haired and blue-eyed, with a narrow intelligent face, serious, even aloof, until the wide smile that held gentleness and compassion as well as humour transformed him, Nick Waring, they said at the Central London Hospital, had a considerable future ahead of him. Sophie, who loved him, was certain of it.

When the telephone rang, he groaned. He was on call that night for the General Surgical Unit. 'Casualty, no doubt,' he commented wearily, reaching for the instrument.

But the call was from Spain, the exchange told him. It turned out to be his stepfather on the line. Or, to be accurate, one of his stepfathers, the property-developer on the Costa Brava. His mother had two marriages behind her, was well into the third. The call was about his young sister, Louise. Could he have her for a week or two?

'Of course,' he said at once.

'Trish is in Rome,' his stepfather explained, 'so she can't keep an eye on her, and I've got meetings in Madrid all week. I've booked the child on a flight to London. If you can take her off at your end, look after her for a bit, that's one problem solved.'

'Put her on the plane, and I'll be there,' Nick promised. 'Heathrow? Tomorrow morning? Right.' He took down details of flight number and E.T.A.

'Thanks, Nick.' His stepfather was clearly relieved. 'Trish said I'd be able to rely on you.' Before Nick had a chance to enquire, belatedly, how they both were, the line had gone dead. Property-developers, he re-marked to Sophie, his blue eyes amused, didn't make their money by unnecessary chat with relatives. 'Louse is coming over,' he added. 'You'll be able to meet her.' He was still noting the Heathrow details in his book when the telephone pealed again. This time it was Casualty. 'I'll have to go across,' he told Sophie regretfully. 'So much for our quiet evening. Looks as though we're in for a busy night. It's the rain. Wet roads.'

She nodded. A small, frail-looking girl with honey-coloured hair that hung straight and gleaming, a peaky face, was apt to arouse the protective instinct in men. Nick Waring had not been the only young sur-geon at the Central who longed to look after her, shelter her for ever.

Appearances, though can be misleading. Sophie was not particularly fragile, certainly not in need of care and protection. Secre-tary to Leo Rosenstein, Assistant Director of the General Surgical Unit at the Central, Sophie ran the unit's administration, not to mention Leo himself, with brisk capability, unflurried in the midst of uproar and the clash of surgical temperament. Now, clear-ing away their coffee cups, she said only, 'I'll see to these, Nick. You get across to Cas.'

'Thanks, love,' he said, held her to him for a moment, and was gone.

In Casualty it was a heavy night. Prolonged rain after drought had made the roads treacherous. All night long, ambulances brought in the injured.

At two o'clock, Nick had to ring Stephen King, his chief, at his home in Hampstead. King came in, not in the best of humours. Even in his younger days, he had never been over-fond of night calls. When he arrived, though, grumbling and impatient as ever, ready for trouble, his surgery was not only impeccable but life-saving.

They were three hours in the theatre, and it was after five when King drove back to Hampstead, and Nick returned to his own flat in St Anne's Square, round the corner from the hospital. With luck, he thought hopefully, he might be left in peace now. The rain had stopped. If he went to bed immediately, he would be able to fit in four hours' sleep before he had to set off for London Airport.

But it wasn't a night for any sort of luck.

The telephone shrilled again almost at once. He sighed, picked it up, listened. 'Right,' he said, 'I'll come over.'

He ran the two blocks. He was lean and

fit, the exercise didn't trouble him, but the account he'd received of the patient did. When he reached Casualty, he liked what he found even less. The patient, a nineteen-year-old driver of a newspaper van, had crashed with a Ford Cortina coming far too fast round a corner on the slippery road. Both drivers had been brought to the Central, but the man from the Cortina had escaped with cuts and bruises, and a possible fracture of the leg that required X-ray. No problems there.

The young van driver, though, was ashen, his pulse rate rising. Nick examined him, confirmed what he'd been told on the telephone, and more. He'd have to call Stephen King back. No alternative. Twice in one night. He wouldn't be pleased.

But King, to give him his due, beyond the first irritated 'What is it *now?*' made no complaint.

'Internal bleeding. I see. Ruptured spleen, you think it might be? After a road accident. Yes. What did you find on examination?'

Nick told him. King asked questions, made a few comments. 'Ballance's sign?' he demanded.

'I'm not sure, sir. Dullness on both sides. My impression is that on the right...' Nick went into details.

'And what about Kehr's sign?' Five in the morning, but he might have been on a teaching round.

'I think that's present, sir. But there's a good deal of bruising, and it's just possible that the pain and tenderness in the left shoulder are due to local injury. Though I doubt it.'

'So do I.' King, as usual, was decisive. 'This sounds like a ruptured spleen to me, too, Waring. Take him to the theatre and go ahead. I'll come in at once, but don't wait for me. Get in without delay and arrest the haemorrhage. I'll be with you as soon as I can make it.' He rang off.

The anaesthetist had gone to bed, he said wearily.

'Sorry, but you'll have to come down here. I think we may have a ruptured spleen. King's coming in, but I want to get the patient on the table *stat.*'

'On my way, laddie.'

He was there before Nick had finished ringing the laboratory for blood, and the patient went direct to the theatre, accompanied by a spiky-haired anaesthetist sporting a nice line in orange pyjamas, inadequately concealed under jeans and sweater.

Scrubbing up, reviewing all he knew and had observed of this particularly operation, Nick recalled in detail the occasion four months ago when he had assisted King to remove a damaged spleen, remembered too how a year back as a house surgeon he had watched Leo Rosenstein and his registrar, Johnnie Clarkson, carry out the same technique. He thought over the measures he'd taken tonight and the possibilities ahead. Would they need to transfuse the patient with his own blood? They could collect it by suction during the operation, filter it in the theatre, use it immediately. They'd have to be prepared to do this, he decided.

Keyed for action, he was ready to make the most of this opportunity. But he had to ask himself if he was being overconfident? This was a man's life in his hands. Suppose he was even a second or two slower than King would have been? Fractionally less sure and certain? No good pretending he was as good as King or Leo Rosenstein. He wasn't. Would the patient be better served if King arrived in time to do the job?

Nick wanted above all to begin. Apprehensive now, as soon as he could go into action he knew he'd be relaxed and calm.

The anaesthetist brought the patient in.

He didn't care for the look of him, he said, and he'd like the end of the table up as far as possible. 'Speed will be of the essence, laddie.'

Nick nodded, cool and remote. An icy determination had taken over. No trace of excitement remained – except perhaps that his eyes shone more vividly blue, though even this might have been the glare of the theatre lighting. 'We won't wait for Mr King, sister.' The atmosphere was taut, the little group, capped, gowned, masked, weary after the long night, was alert now, fatigue forgotten. Not one of them – patients, surgeons, nurses, technicians or porters, had reached thirty. Most were under twenty-five.

The table was tilted, the patient covered. Nick made the first incision. Everything left him except concentration on the demands of the emergency surgery.

'You were dead right, Nick,' the house surgeon commented. 'Just as well we got him up here at the gallop, wasn't it?'

Nick grunted. One of the difficult moments had come. He had to get his hand round the damaged spleen itself, to hold it safely while he probed and separated, dissected and divided the ligament. Neat, accurate, methodical as he had to be throughout, he could never allow himself to forget he had to be fast, too.

'Excellent, Waring, excellent. You're doing very well. Just as we thought, eh? You'd better carry on. I'll give you a hand.'

He was thankful to hear King's voice, though he hadn't even been aware of his arrival. However, his assistance was to prove distinctly more alarming than his absence had been. Operating under King's critical eye was always a hazard, of course, but one to which Nick had grown accustomed. Tonight, though, he found this complicated surgery on a deteriorating patient – a race against time in any case – was to be punctuated by weary sighs and a barrage of sniping comment. His chief, evidently feeling that his earlier – and unprecedented – words of encouragement might easily go to his registrar's head, reverted to his more usual fault-finding irritability. Between them, though, they saved the patient.

Altogether a night and a half. It had followed a demanding day, and he was exhausted when he reached the house in St Anne's Square again. As he climbed the stairs, Sophie came hurtling down from her flat in the attics.

'Hello,' he said, surprised. 'You on your

way in?' He frowned. 'It can't be as late as that, surely?'

She glanced at her watch. 'Ten to nine, I'm afraid.'

'Hell. I was going to have some breakfast and a bath. But I must be at London Airport by ten.'

'Oh, Nick, what a shame.' Sophie's green eyes were wide with concern. 'Surely you can…'

'Not to worry, love. I'll have some coffee when I get there.'

They left the house together – Sophie as blonde as Nick was dark, her pale and shining head reaching only to his shoulder. He took her hand, swung it affectionately as they walked along. At the tube station they separated, Sophie going on to the hospital, while Nick plunged down into the underground network. He carried with him the picture of Sophie's fragile beauty, and alongside it now Louise's dark brilliance. They said she was turning out to be as beautiful as her mother, Trish, who, dark-haired, with huge brown eyes and soft wide mouth, had always had a touch of magic, embodied in her slim loveliness something of any man's dreams.

That, of course, had been the trouble. Any

man would leap at the chance of taking her on, and Trish was only too often ready for excitement and a new love. Five years earlier, when she had left the painter who had been her second husband, and gone to live in Spain before marrying her third, she had taken the twelve-year-old Louise with her. The child of Trish's first marriage, Louise until then had been brought up by her grandparents, Matthew and Joanna Waring, who had looked after Nick from babyhood.

Nick, who had three stepfathers, had no legal father. Trish had only just left school when he had been born, his father a sixth-former taking his A-levels. Nick had never met him, never even heard his name. He hardly knew Trish either. She had vanished from home before he was two, returned only at irregular intervals (from, needless to say, an irregular life, though he hadn't been aware of this at the time). She brought with her, in due course, a small baby. Louise. Nick had adored the tiny creature they told him was his half-sister, had taken, too, a detailed interest – possibly the forerunner of his later commitment to medicine – in the methods required to care for her. He assisted expertly at bathtime and even nappy-changing, was occasionally allowed to feed her himself. Much better, he had told Matthew seriously, than a kitten or a puppy, even. Matthew, equally seriously, had agreed with him, gone away to enjoy with Joanna one of the few laughs either of them had out of their daughter's affairs and their consequences.

When Trish finally left her first husband for a painter in Cornwall, she took Louise with her. Once in Cornwall, though, she found her somewhat of a problem, and a year later, with another child on the way she sent Louise home to Joanna. Silent and large-eyed when she reached Cheam, in a neighbour's car, Louise, who had grasped long ago that she was a nuisance to her mother and had guessed she was being sent away in some sort of disgrace, was relieved to find the familiar Joanna at the end of her journey. Nick, too. She didn't adapt easily, of course, but Joanna was at last beginning to hope that she was settling down when Trish appeared with the new baby.

Only for a brief visit, but enough to upset Louise. Totally demoralized, she took refuge in complete withdrawal, refusing to speak, refusing to eat, staring woodenly from wide, alarmed brown eyes. In the end it had been Nick who brought her out of it, offering her, with a schoolboy's confidence, a midnight feast, bought especially out of his pocket money, and guaranteed, he had estimated, to cheer anyone up. Mars bar, Coke and crisps, plus a bag of sherbet. Louse had come to life, had wept tempestuously in his arms. 'Nobody wants me,' she had hiccupped despairingly. 'And Mummy's got a new baby now.'

'I want you, Lulu,' he had assured her, had repeated it until she had at last believed him. The Mars bar and the Coke bore him out, too. He'd spent his own money on her. Greatly relieved, she sat on his knee eating them up, let him tuck her up in bed, went straight off to sleep. The next day she had been herself again, functioning normally, eating like a horse, and following Nick everywhere.

This therapeutic feasting had been re-enacted at intervals throughout her childhood, never failed to put new heart into her. Only the nature of the feasts had changed over the years. This thought brought Nick up with a jerk. The present-day Louise would presumably expect wine, candlelight and throbbing music to celebrate their first evening together. He must take them both out tonight, Louise and Sophie. Take them somewhere expensive.

Sophie. In the rattling, swaying train, worn out after the hard night, hungry too, he smiled triumphantly. Sophie was his. Her beauty and her love were for him. He'd had a lonely struggle before he qualified, but he'd finally made it. And now the good days were here, and Sophie to share them with him. His career was more of a success than he'd ever dared to hope.

He and Sophie might be able to marry before the year was out. He had the flat in St Anne's Square, they'd have a home of their own.

A home for Louise, too.

At the airport she flung herself into his arms, screeching lovingly. Nearly as tall now as he was himself, she was astoundingly beautiful. Sophisticated, too, if looks were anything to go by. Seventeen only, but she would have passed easily for twenty, he thought. Amazing to think this was the little sister who had trotted round behind him in the small house in suburban Cheam.

Already she was gabbling fast and happily. 'Oh Nickie darling, what bliss to see you again. What a simply super surprise.' She rattled on non-stop, about Trish in Rome, about her stepfather driving her to the airport, about her rushed and unexpected packing, and the passengers she'd talked to on the plane.

He listened affectionately, but soon began to notice, clinical detachment overriding his own delight, that she was over-excited, a little too feverish. Even for Louise, prone to exaggerated moods. But he suspected nothing like the brutal truth.

CHAPTER TWO

LOUISE

Louise was on heroin. A death sentence, in Nick's eyes. Not in hers, of course. 'Only a small amount, Nickie, truly. The thing is, though, I must have it. But I knew you'd be able to see about that.'

The first step, at least, was straightforward. He rang through to the drug treatment centre attached – though as distantly as the parent hospital could reasonably make it – to the Central. Paul Worsley, a Central registrar several years Nick's senior, was on duty there. 'Bring her round immediately,' he said.

When they arrived Paul saw Louise alone, spent over an hour with her. Afterwards he spent half an hour with Nick. But like any other shattered relative, Nick found he could barely remember what Paul had said, other than that Louise would last out until the morning on what he'd given her, that Nick must bring her round to the Centre at 10 a.m. 'Can you get someone to cover for you?' he asked.

Nick nodded. 'No difficulty there.' As horrified as he was himself, his friends rallied instantly.

No backing, though, came from his stepfather. 'I knew that lot she was going around with were no good to her,' he said, shocked at the news Nick had telephoned through. 'I warned Trish again and again, she can't say I didn't. But I never expected anything as bad as this. What on earth she's going to say – I'll have to get on to her in Rome, I suppose.' He sounded distinctly unwilling to do this. 'No,' he decided. 'You get on to her. I'll give you the number.'

Nick took it down. As soon as he'd repeated it back the line went dead. Typical, he thought, remembering the previous conversation and its equally abrupt termination. But three days later a letter came from his stepfather, informing Nick of the fact that by then he'd unearthed for himself. He and Trish were divorcing. Louise was Trish's child, the letter understandably pointed out, and in future Trish would have to be responsible for her.

Only, of course, Trish had never been responsible for anyone or anything, least of all when she was engrossed in a new love. In the past there'd been Joanna to turn to, today there was Nick. She reiterated unhelpfully that Louise had never been anything but impossibly difficult. However, thank goodness, Nick had always been the one person who could handle her, and fortunately, too, he was a doctor and would know exactly what to do. What? No, obviously she couldn't have Louise in Rome with her. Not now, of all times. What could he be thinking of? He must get her into hospital, or something.

Nick had never felt so inadequate, so helpless. There seemed nothing he could do.

His work began to suffer. He'd find himself staring into space, trying to deny what he knew to be fact, Louise's addiction. In a ward round, he'd find he'd lost the thread, was worrying about Louise, asking himself what the hell he could do to halt the inexorable progress of the heroin addict, the insidious descent to inevitable death. His friends began to tire of conversations that started out as case discussions about patients in the wards, only to turn into yet another of Nick's monologues about his sister.

In the theatre alone he could find relief from his anxiety. Here, in the quiet disciplined environment that he loved, his concentration remained unimpaired, head and hands interacted as they'd always done. He was thankful to be able to escape for a few hours into the straightforward demands of surgery, to work his way through King's list, secure from interruption.

Finally, he put Louise into a private clinic. There was no other practical solution. He borrowed a car, drove her down to Berkshire, left her there. She cried bitterly, begged him to stay with her, promised him she'd follow the treatment, try to free herself from the drug, if only he'd take her home again. 'I'm sure I can, Nickie. Truly. It's only that it was so awful in Spain just recently, you've no idea. Everyone was so miserable, and I didn't know what on earth was going to happen next, except that it was all going to break up, everyone would be gone. Well, I was right, wasn't I? You see? And these people were so sweet to me, they said I'd feel much better if I just had a shot. And I did. It was the answer to everything. When I was on it, I knew I could cope. Only I never for a moment expected it to be so fearfully expensive, or so difficult to get hold of. But I do promise you I will try, if you think it's so important.'

She did try, too, and his worries began to recede. Perhaps it would be all right, perhaps her addiction was a brief, insolated incident. He went down to see her once a week – he had to be firm about having his day off, of course, which was unpopular with King, but his colleagues covered for him loyally.

He lay awake at night, though. Louise was so young still. To be hooked on heroin at seventeen was ominous, he knew that. Yet she was no more than a child, after all. She hadn't known what she was doing.

'None of them know what they're doing,' Paul said bleakly.

Staring into the darkness, Nick remembered this, but determined somehow he would break the deadly chain, see Louise freed from dependence on the drug.

But that there was a price to be paid, and not in cash alone, he was to find out quickly enough.

Paul was the first to warn him. 'You have a duty to yourself as well as Louise,' he reminded him more than once. 'Don't jeopardize your own future for a junkie who'll only let you down in the end.'

Nick flinched. To hear Louise described casually as a junkie horrified him.

Paul had persevered. 'I'm sorry, Nick, but you'd better face it sooner rather than later. Don't sacrifice yourself.' He had seen too many relatives tearing themselves apart trying to salvage hopeless addicts. He had heard some of the talk at the Central, too.

'I'm sorry for poor old Nick,' they were saying now. 'It's a tragedy about that sister of his. But if he doesn't look out, he's going to be the one to suffer.'

'He's the nicest of blokes – and used to be the most hard-working. But now – he's no memory, he's late for every appointment. One of these days he'll go too far, be in real trouble.'

'It's bad luck he's working for Steve King.'

'That miserable old slave-driver wouldn't lift a finger if Nick were dying on his feet.'

'Which he's beginning to look as if he is.'

Giles Stanstead, who had been a student with him, spoke to him. 'You can't let everything go like this, simply because of Louise, you know. Can't she go to her mother, for heaven's sake?'

'Won't have her. In the middle of a divorce.'

'Look, Nick, you're getting a bad reputation. Don't take risks with your future.'

The trouble was, Giles said, in the common room later, Nick didn't seem to grasp how quickly his career could be finished if he went on like this. 'You've got to be single-minded to hold down a surgical post here. Or suddenly you're through. Before you know what's hit you, you'll meet yourself coming out.'

'You have to make a choice, and stick to it. Hospital or family.'

'It's true. You can't compromise, take on a post as surgical registrar at any teaching hospital and expect to run a private life as well.'

'Least of all when your chief is Stephen King,' someone added sourly.

'Nick will have to steel himself, and send the girl back to her mother, whether she wants her or not. It's the only solution.'

Even Sophie began pressing him to send Louise to Trish in Rome as soon as her treatment at the clinic was complete. 'You've seen her over the worst part. Now Trish must take a hand.'

'She's not over the worst part. She has it ahead of her. Staying off the drug is the crunch.'

'Looking after Louise is a full-time job, anyway, and you can't take it on.'

'I don't see how I can, either,' he agreed. 'But you don't know what you can do until you try, do you? In any case, apart from the fact that Trish had refused to have her, I know perfectly well that if she went to Rome, in that set-up, she'd be back on heroin inside a week.' He shivered. 'Anything to prevent that.'

In the end Louise was booked into a residential course in creative arts in the depths of Suffolk. Not a very brilliant move, and it cost the earth. Nick dug into capital again – the small amount left to him by Matthew and Joanna was dwindling fast – wrote to Trish to report progress and ask for a financial contribution. He had no reply.

Louise stuck the course for no more than six weeks, appeared one afternoon in the flat in St Anne's Square. She'd been in Suffolk for an eternity, she told him. She couldn't stand the people, and she might as well have been back at school. 'Or in the army. Positively regimented, we were.'

In spite of himself, Nick's lips had twitched. The improbable notion of Louise under army discipline had its appeal.

'And the teaching was hopeless. I know more about painting and design than those morons. Anyway, Nickie, I can come home now, can't I? Don't you think I deserve it, after the effort I've made?'

She'd promised to attend lectures regularly, take a part-time job too.

Once in the flat, though, it soon became

plain that she expected to be the centre of his existence. If his life failed to revolve around her, there was immediate trouble. Sophie did her best to help him out, but this only led to jealous outbursts and scenes. Nick had to face the knowledge that Louise was trying to drive a wedge between him and Sophie. What's more, she was not entirely unsuccessful. He hardly dared bring Sophie into the flat now, knowing that if he did Louise would be at her worst, would make Sophie thoroughly uncomfortable. He began to have some sympathy with Trish and his stepfather, gone to ground in Rome and Spain respectively, he could see exactly why.

Finally he went for Louse, ticked her off unmistakably, in true elder brother fashion, read her the riot act. She cried so miserably that he was ashamed of himself for his bad temper. But she admitted, too, that she'd behaved impossibly, begged him to invite Sophie in that very minute. She'd make it up to her, she swore. She had never meant to be horrid, she never would again.

So Sophie came to supper. Louise behaved angelically, was charming, thoughtful, attentive. Thoroughly civilized and agreeable. Nick could hardly believe his eyes, concluded he should throw his weight around more often.

The next evening, though, when he came in from the hospital, Louise was missing. She didn't appear until after three in the morning. Stoned. What on, he couldn't discover, nor where she had obtained her supply of whatever she'd taken. How she had found the means to pay, though, was immediately clear. His transistor had vanished.

After this, he took to dashing into the flat whenever he had half an hour free, simply to see if she was there, what she was up to. If he was late back in the evening, though, she'd have gone. Unless he could track her down, he wouldn't see her until the early hours. But if he did the rounds, he'd usually meet up with her sooner or later.

Slowly but surely, though, her range extended. Soon, night after night, he found himself hunting for her in half a dozen neighbourhood pubs, scrutinizing groups at street corners, entering sleazy, down-at-heel discotheques, or the cafés where local drop-outs gathered. Sometimes she was obviously relieved when he reappeared, left with him thankfully. At others, though, she refused to come home. Sometimes, of course, he wasn't able to trace her. And always he dreaded the day when he wouldn't find her in any of these haunts, when he'd have to begin searching the lavatories where the junkies went for their fixes. He knew too much about drug addicts and their despairing lives, too much about the spots where they gathered, the inevitable death lying in wait for them, so young and yet so old. Anything to keep Louise away from that world.

But at the Central to complete your hours of duty and then disappear wasn't good enough. Even his contemporaries grew tired of his eagerness to finish and be away, his regular requests for someone to cover for him. When he was on call he'd never yet failed to find someone to stand in for him, but they were becoming increasingly restive. Between them, they were having to run his job for him, they told one another grudgingly.

His unreliability became a by-word. Worst of all, Stephen King complained that he never knew whom he would find on the end of the line when he wanted young Waring. Anyone, it seemed, other than Waring himself. Thoroughly unsatisfactory. What sort of a registrar was that? He took to ringing simply to check. 'Mr King here. I want Mr Waring.'

'I'm sorry, sir, Mr Stanstead is taking Mr

Waring's calls. Shall I put you through to him?'

'No. Tell Mr Waring to ring me as soon as he's available.'

It happened too often. This was, after all, the Central, where competition for registrars' posts was keen. Any number of eager young men were ready to step into his shoes.

King complained to Hugh Alexander, the Resident Surgical Officer. This put the R.S.O. in a spot. He knew the cause of Nick's behaviour, but he'd been told in confidence, and he didn't think he ought to pass the information on to King. To one of the other consultants, he might have taken a chance and explained the exact situation. But Stephen King was such a tricky devil, he couldn't foresee what line he'd take. If he learnt that Nick's sister, living with him in a Central flat, was a heroin addict, that might well be the end for Nick. 'He has family problems just now, sir,' was the most he felt it safe to say. It was more than enough.

'Family problems?' King repeated, not only disagreeably but with incredulity, rather as though the R.S.O. had announced Waring was having difficulty with little three-headed men on flying saucers. 'Family problems? His first duty is to the patients in this hospital. If he can't spare time away from his *family* to attend to them, the sooner he resigns in favour of someone who's prepared to give time to the care of the sick the better. Am I supposed to do his work for him, then, while he attends to his domestic affairs?'

'I'll have a word with him, sir,' the R.S.O. promised, harassed. He had Nick on the mat the next day. Hugh Alexander was a kind man, but at present he had more work than anyone else would have been able to get through. He was sorry for Nick, and said so. But he was sorry for himself, too. With Leo Rosenstein still away in the States and Lord Mummery newly retired, the General Surgical Unit was understaffed. The extra burden fell on the R.S.O. And, now of all times, when he was under pressure, one of his best young registrars had to run into these difficulties, become totally useless, as well as bringing Steve King down on him like a ton of bricks. Alexander chewed Nick into very small pieces indeed. Perhaps that would bring him to his senses. 'It left me feeling every sort of a heel,' he explained to the Resident Medical Officer, his opposite number on the medical side, that evening. 'He looks exhausted and haunted, you know, white and thoroughly nervy. He's going through hell, I should say. What on earth am I going to do about him?

'Nothing,' the R.M.O. said placidly. 'Nothing at all. Or you'll end up white and haunted yourself. Waring's problems are for Waring. You know that as well as I do, Alex. Your problem is to see that the surgery in this hospital is maintained at Central standards. That's what you're here for. Not to set up as some sort of social worker.'

'Simple, isn't it?' Alexander asked, and sighed.

'Simple. Also correct,' the R.M.O. assured him firmly.

When Nick's contract came up for renewal, the R.S.O. expressed his doubts. 'I'm afraid Waring is not too reliable just at present,' he began, hating himself for the damning words. But the R.M.O. had been right. His duty was to the hospital first and last, always had been. Not to any individual member of the junior staff.

King had exploded before he'd been able to continue. 'Not too reliable,' he had repeated with blistering scorn. 'Utterly unreliable would be nearer the mark. Time after time, when I need him, I find...' He instanced what he found in elaborate detail.

'Do you know, only last night when I rang…'

The outcome was inevitable. Nick Waring's contract was not renewed. Giles Stanstead was appointed as Stephen King's registrar from the first of the following month.

CHAPTER THREE

SOPHIE

Even now, he couldn't believe it, couldn't take it in, as, in shabby jeans and roll-neck sweater, he stood at the window, watched the big removal van turn into the square, come lumbering round. In spite of all that people had said, he'd never imagined it coming to this. He'd continued to assume that somehow he'd be able to hold things together. But suddenly, overnight, his career at the Central had crumbled.

Only a year earlier he'd stood for the first time in these high rooms with their tall Georgian windows overlooking the square. Sophie had been with him, he'd felt a glow of achievement and hope, a quiet confidence in their future.

No Sophie beside him now, with her frail blonde charm, coupled with the crisp down-to-earth comments that were so typical of her. Leaving Sophie was the hardest part of going. Harder even than the loss of his job,

39

of his future as a surgeon. For his career, he knew, was ended. Once you'd failed at the Central, you were finished.

Louise didn't understand this, of course. 'You'll be able to find a job, won't you?' she asked, anxious, her brown eyes appealing.

'Oh yes, we shan't starve,' he'd agreed brusquely. He ought to reassure her, but just then he couldn't. He hadn't bargained for the wrecking of his career, least of all for the separating from Sophie.

His eyes sombre, he went down to open the door to the removal men.

For the next few hours the flat reverberated with their activity. Then they had gone, taking the furniture into store. Nick and Louise were left in the bare, echoing flat, with only their personal possessions and a few household necessities, Nick's medical case and his surgical textbooks.

Not so long ago, he'd dreamed of being some sort of surgical phenomenon. Nonsense, of course. But until recently he'd genuinely had a decent chance of making a respectable career for himself in surgery, he knew. Now all he'd managed to land was a month's locum in the casualty department at Eversholt's, the half-abandoned hospital down between the railway lines. A place that was little more than a joke at the Central. A bad joke at that.

Because he had only this month's post, he'd had to take what he could find in the way of accommodation, and what he could find turned out to be a tired old flat on the borders of Camden Town and Chalk Farm. Like Eversholt's, within sound of the railway.

Louise drifted round it, making a genuine attempt to cheer him up. 'It's quite fun, Nickie, no need to be so dreadfully glum and down in the mouth. And it's only for a month after all. When you've done as much moving as I have, you won't take it to heart so much.' She wandered over to the window, peered down into the crowded evening traffic. 'By the way,' she said, glancing at the huge green-dialled, green-strapped watch she wore, 'Peregrine will be around any minute. He's taking me out for a meal. To recover from the move.'

'Hadn't you better change, then?'

'Oh, Nickie, do you think I should?'

She looked a mess, he thought, in a long skirt of a dark cotton print, flounced and flowing, and a plain blue shirt that in fact belonged to him, with the sleeves rolled up. Her dark hair hung loose, falling about her face, her fingers were loaded with the heavy barbaric rings she adored. Above all, she was grubby, as was only to be expected after the move. The skirt was smeared, a great streak of dust lay across her shirt, her nails were broken and grimy.

'Why don't you have a bath?' he suggested.

'No time.' She twitched the skirt, pushed her shirt in at the waistband, combed her hair with her fingers. 'I'll do as I am, I expect.'

Nick had to admit she probably would. In an odd way she remained beautiful still, even had a touch of weird splendour.

'There he is,' she remarked from the window. 'I'll go down and let him in.'

Peregrine was a photographer who had met Louise in one of her discotheques, or so they both said, and had begun to use her in features for fashion magazines. He had paid her well when he did so, though the money slipped easily between her fingers. They came into the shabby room together. 'Well,' Peregrine paused, exhaled clouds of smoke. 'This is a bit of a come-down, wouldn't you say?' His eyes darted round the room appraisingly, as he flicked ash anywhere. A head shorter than Louise, lithe and quick, with black shoulder-length hair, beads round his neck and rings on his fingers, a dark blue suede shirt, matching suede jeans flaring over stack-heeled boots, he brought tension with him, coupled with an alert, lively intelligence. 'Definitely a comedown, dears.'

Nick knew it was no more than the truth, but he was infuriated to hear Peregrine point it out. 'Temporary,' he said shortly.

'Oh, now he's offended, Lulu. I meant no personal criticism, I do assure you, Nick.' His eyes travelled still, carrying out an inventory. 'But really, I must say, it does begin to verge on the sordid.'

Nick thought it more than verged. It was sordid. He sighed. Why argue with Peregrine? He was right, blast him. 'Yeah, I'd say that too. But it's a roof.'

'That does have its advantages, I'm bound to agree. Come along then, Lulu babe, if Nick's lost his job and is joining the bread line, you'd better be seen around in the right places with Uncle. Let's get going.'

As soon as they'd gone, Nick cleaned the squalid flat throughout, working on until pangs of hunger reminded him how late it was, that he'd had no more than a sandwich and a cup of coffee since breakfast.

Supper. Neither he nor Louise had done any shopping, and when he investigated in the kitchen all they had in stock was tinned tuna or beans, a piece of stale cheddar, a few Ryvita. He'd have to go out. And the thought he'd been avoiding could be resisted no longer. Why not take Sophie out to supper?

He'd ring her.

He ceased to care about the sordid flat, even the dead-end job didn't matter. His spirits rose blithely. He'd ring Sophie.

The telephone was out on the landing. At least, though, even in this hole, it was close by his own door, so that he could be reached instantly.

He pulled himself up. Reached for what, he demanded bitterly? There'd be no more urgent calls to the Central's theatres for him. He was simply another locum casualty officer at Eversholt's, from 9 a.m. to 6 p.m. daily. The department was closed in the evening and overnight patients referred to other hospitals. No one would be ringing him here.

Never mind. He would be ringing Sophie. He found change, went out to the landing, dialed the familiar number.

But the telephone rang on, in what he recognized must be an empty flat. He could not bear to put it down and face the reality, allowed it to ring far longer than was reasonable. Finally he replaced it, went back into his own flat. No supper with Sophie.

He went into the dingy kitchen, opened a tin of beans, poured water on instant coffee. Life didn't stop, he reminded himself coldly, merely because he'd left the Central. As Leo Rosenstein's secretary, Sophie met all the residents on the surgical side, the consultants too. Any of them might have taken her out for a meal. He had no right to ask her to share his problems now. The sacrifice he'd been forced to make for Louise was his alone. Sophie must not be involved in it. He must expect her to go out and about, be prepared for her to lose touch with him.

This was what he told himself. But as soon as he'd swallowed the beans and coffee, he went out to the landing again, rang her number a second time. No reply. He had to accept it, she was out with someone else.

Sophie was down in his empty flat, talking to Giles Stanstead who was taking it over, in addition to Nick's former post. He'd told her of this, somewhat edgily, a few days earlier.

'Nick's flat too?' Sophie had repeated

blankly. They'd all known about the post, of course, for a month now.

'Someone's going to live in it,' Giles pointed out. 'So why not me?'

Why not indeed? Sophie had no answer. But the news came as a jolt. She had not been prepared for this swift changeover, had not foreseen the possibility that now instead of Nick two floors below there would be Giles.

He was regarding her somewhat anxiously, she saw. Had he understood that her thoughts remained with Nick?

A friendly bear of a man, with chubby features and twinkling eyes, fair curling hair, broad shoulders, and big capable hands, Giles, though a friend of Nick's from student days, was his opposite. Where Giles was ebullient, trendy, flamboyant, Nick had been serious, conservative, unostentatious. Until lately, though, Sophie had thought of him as quietly elegant. Recently, of course, with all the pressures on him, he had taken to wandering about in old jeans, dirty sweaters, his shoes unpolished, his hair straggling over his collar. Sophie didn't herself object to him like this – in some ways he seemed far more approachable – but she knew it had harmed him at the Central. Meanwhile Giles, to everyone's amazement – as a student he had been hairy, rugged, colourful – began to tone down the flamboyance, was to be seen in formal suits and subdued ties. His hair no longer curled on his shoulders, he'd shaved off his beard, sported long side-burns instead. All this restraint had paid off. Stephen King, when the crisis came, had looked on him with favour.

Tonight he'd invited Sophie out to celebrate his new appointment. It would cheer her up, he told her. When he'd called for her, he'd unexpectedly steered her into the empty flat on their way to dinner at the extravagant restaurant he'd chosen. But he'd only succeeded in upsetting her, he could see that, and cursed inwardly. He was anxious for her to forget Nick. 'Too many ghosts today, are there, duckie?' he inquired. He had no subtlety, was often tactless. 'Wait until I've some furniture in, slapped a bit of paint on. That'll liven the place up.'

He was right about that, Sophie had to admit, a bare four days later, as she wiped the last smear of paint off the floor. Giles was roaring away in the kitchen, opening bottles, cracking ice, making a special drink for his housewarming.

Sophie threw a final amazed glance round

the room. Giles had transformed it. Gone was Nick's friendly old flat, distinguished mainly by the Georgian proportions of walls and high sashed windows.

Over the weekend, Giles had been to a couple of cash and carry furniture warehouses, and had emerged triumphantly with a round table and six rush-seated chairs stained green. These stood now in the short arm of the L-shaped living room, where he had painted the walls a deep navy blue. Up at the wide end of the room, where the two tall windows looked southwards on to the square, the walls had become emerald green. Here he'd placed wide chrome chairs and settee, covered in blue cord, and two huge glass-topped coffee tables, while Nick's yellow Afghan rug had been superseded by a thick hairy white rectangle. The effect was not only dramatic, but curiously enough lavish, even expensive, though in fact Giles had spent amazingly little.

Up in her own flat, Sophie showered and changed fast. She found – a little to her surprise, since she would have said that parties were not her strong point – that she was looking forward to Giles' housewarming. He'd like her to dress up for it too, so she poured herself into a long slinky oriental print that clung to her hips, swirled round her long legs, and might have been designed for Giles' new décor, with its purple and gold, blue, green and brilliant turquoise, blending and intricate. All she had left to do was brush out her straight blonde hair, drench herself in the Arpège that Giles had given her last Christmas, and go down.

A roar of sound rose up to meet her. While she'd been changing she'd heard the car doors slamming in the street below, the talk on the stairs, the welcoming cries. Now the front door was wide open, she could see straight into the crowded flat. The thick Danish candles were alight, the drink was going round in the dark green tumblers Giles had acquired for a song. The record player thumped ecstatically, and half the resident staff at the Central, it seemed, had deserted the wards and come to warm Giles' flat for him.

Competent as ever, Giles fielded her neatly, before she'd lost impetus. 'Sophie, there's my girl. I was going to come up and search for you if you'd been five minutes longer.' He surveyed her, whistled appreciatively. 'Duckie, I don't know how you do it. Ten minutes ago there you were, grovelling on the floor in ancient jeans mopping

49

up my paint spills, and now look at you.' Still with an arm round her shoulders, he bellowed above the uproar, 'Here's Sophie. Now we can really get going.'

In all this approval Sophie bloomed. Her green eyes shone, her pale features took on the ethereal beauty that had won Nick's heart. The party went with a swing, and Sophie with it. When at ten in the evening Giles insisted on leaving the flat's chaos behind and going out for a meal at Giovanni's, opposite the Central, before he did his final round, they both knew the housewarming had been a success. They relived it as they ate, Giles told her in some detail of other improvements he proposed for the flat. Over coffee he began to discuss his next step on the road to personal fulfilment – the car he was going to buy.

Giles was on the up and up, Sophie thought. Yet as a student he had been mediocre only, whereas Nick had been brilliant. As soon as he had qualified he had taken the top jobs in general surgery, became house surgeon first to Leo Rosenstein, then to Lord Mummery himself. Yet in a few short months she had seen him throw his future away. In the common rooms they were saying now there would never be another post for Nick Waring at the Central. Apart from anything else, he'd made an enemy of King. Fatal.

'Poor old Nick,' Giles remarked, out of the blue. Had he read her thoughts? Sophie caught out, eyed him warily. 'A pity he couldn't have been with us this evening. I could do with some advice from him – as well as a lot of the luck he didn't have. Poor old Nick,' he repeated, a little guiltily this time. He was on edge about having taken his job and his flat, knew very well he was going to try as hard as he knew to take over Nick's girl as well. 'I'll need all the help I can muster, if I'm to hold this job down,' he commented, hoping to gain Sophie's sympathy. 'Not as bright as Nick, not by a long chalk.'

Relief flooded Sophie. At last someone was prepared to speak well of Nick. Too many people had been running him down to her, blaming him for the ruin of his career, warning her off him. 'Oh Giles,' she exclaimed sadly. 'Need he have gone? Need it have come to that?'

But Giles failed her. 'Brought it on himself,' he said bluntly. 'He should have ditched Louise and kept off pot.'

'Nick never smoked pot in his life,' Sophie was instantly furious.

Giles loved Sophie's great green eyes set in her pale face, looked into them longingly. Unfortunately they flashed angry defiance back. What he wanted to do this evening was to hold her hand safely in his, go on looking into her eyes, tell her about himself, his hopes and fears in the new job. Instead he had to sit here discussing poor old Nick, instilling the facts of contemporary life into the guileless Sophie.

'I'm afraid he did, you know,' he said firmly. He could see she wasn't going to accept it, but he had to try and convince her. For her own good. 'Didn't you *smell* it, apart from anything else?' he demanded.

'That was Louise,' Sophie said. She was as sure of her facts as he was of his.

Giles set his jaw, began to explain to Sophie, who knew it already, the insidious effects of smoking pot, together with his own conviction that Nick as well as Louise had taken to it. He had strong views, made stronger by what he had recently watched happen to Nick. 'It just shows what a mistake it is to have anything to do with the drug scene,' he said. Smugly, Sophie thought, experiencing a sudden desire to hit him. 'I daresay poor old Nick thought all he was doing was putting up with Louise's habit of rolling a joint now and again – though why he tolerated that I can't understand – but if you ask me he soon tried the experience out for himself. And no doubt he found it took the edge off his troubles. God knows he had enough of those, poor bloke. But it was the beginning of the end, wasn't it?'

Sophie, determined to keep her cool, began cautiously. 'All that you say about pot, of course, is only what my father has been saying for years.' She paused.

Since her father was a world-famous neurologist, Giles was more gratified by this information than he would otherwise have been if compared by a beautiful blonde to her aged parent.

'But,' Sophie went on more confidently, 'it isn't in the least like Nick. He's the last person to try anything of that sort.'

Giles stuck to his guns. 'You can't ignore symptoms, Sophie. Think how his work deteriorated – his appearance, too.'

'Louise,' Sophie repeated.

Giles decided she was refusing to face the obvious. 'People are always amazed when someone they know takes to drugs,' he said kindly. 'Not him, they say, of all people.' He patted her hand reassuringly.

Sophie shook her head, removed her hand.

Giles saw he was getting nowhere. In any case, he hadn't taken Sophie out to talk interminably about Nick's troubles. He changed the subject, made her smile in spite of herself with a sly story against his new chief. Stephen King, of course, was recognized to be touchy, blown up with precarious self-esteem. This had been inadvertently – and quite innocently – punctured by a new house surgeon. The story, amusing in any case – the residents had been splitting their sides for days – was well told by Giles, who had quite a gift for anecdote, and he soon had Sophie falling about helplessly.

In the weeks that followed she found herself spending good few of her evenings with him. Once they drove to the coast for a meal. With his new contract safely in his possession, Giles had bought the car he'd talked about, a yellow Triumph Spitfire, low and fast. He was delighted to take Sophie out in it, show them both off, his bird and his Spitfire. His time off was limited, though. He was concentrating on success in his new post. It was more of a struggle than he had anticipated, and he soon had to admit to himself that he had no hopes of touching Leo Rosenstein's heights. Or even, to be honest, the heights Nick could have aspired to if he'd been able to stay the course. His new post demanded all and more than he had to give it, and he was thankful, during his brief time off duty, to be able to turn to Sophie.

So the days went by, and after the first week, hardly anyone spoke of Nick. They all seemed to have forgotten his existence. His absence, though, left Sophie with a gap that continued to ache painfully. Each day she expected him to ring. But no word came.

However, she was not a girl to sit down, wring her hands and try to forget him. When three weeks had gone by with no call from Nick, she told Barbie Henderson, who shared the attic flat with her, that she'd be out the following evening. 'As soon as I can get away, I'm going down to Eversholt's to see what's happening to Nick, how he's getting on,' she explained. 'He's only got another week of that locum to run, and I want to find out what he's going to do afterwards.' Ready to leave for her office in the surgical block, she was business-like and trim in polo-neck sweater, tweed skirt, high suede boots. Pouring herself a final cup of coffee, she drank it standing. 'Of course, he may be going to do another one there. I imagine they must be short-staffed most of the time.'

Barbie, who didn't care for any of this, came out now from behind the paper where she had been hiding her dismay. 'Whether he stays on or not rather depends on how he's done during these last three weeks, doesn't it?' she inquired crisply. General Theatre Sister at the Central, she had liked Nick, had admired his work. But she had no time for registrars who slacked, whatever their problems, and was worried stiff to find that Sophie remained involved with him. Barbie had been hoping Sophie was growing attached to Giles, who, though he might be a bit thick, was steady-going and reliable, would stand by her and look after her for a lifetime. 'Even Eversholt's presumably like their casualty officers to be available in the department from time to time.' No point in mincing words. If Sophie was hankering after Nick still, she had better be reminded of the facts behind his departure from the Central.

Sophie made no direct reply, merely put her cup down on the saucer with a slight crash, and dashed out of the room, saying only 'Must fly now. See you.'

So much for that. Barbie, who had the morning off, cleared away breakfast, had a leisurely bath and washed her hair, brooding the entire time about Sophie and Nick. She didn't care for the set-up. Something had to be done. In fact, the moment had come to bring Leo into the picture. No doubt about it.

Barbie had known Leo Rosenstein for years. She had been a student nurse when he had been a very new house surgeon. Leo had caused a commotion when he first appeared in the theatres at Central – was continuing to cause it, for that matter.

From the beginning, of course, they had all seen he was going to be outstandingly good. But he remained now what he had been when he first entered the doors of the medical school. A fat boisterous barrow boy from the slums. He had kept his thick fruity voice. His thick fruity figure, too. But alongside his surgical ability he had poise now, coupled with immense skill in management. After his years as Resident Surgical Officer, the top surgical post before consultancy, he had gone into old Mummery's firm. Leo Rosenstein, of all people, on Lord Mummery's firm. The Central had rocked. A tribute not only to his outstanding surgery, but also, as they recognized, to his personal qualities.

For Leo was Leo. He could – and did – go anywhere, join anything he had a mind to join. By this time, the Central would hardly have been surprised if he had suddenly surfaced as Colonel-in-Chief of the Coldstream Guards. The Guards, the Central would have agreed, were lucky to get him.

Barbie was his theatre sister, saw more of him than anyone except his house surgeon and Sophie. After his list that afternoon, when they were downing tea thankfully, she said, 'Sometime I wanted to have a chat, if we could. About Sophie. There's a little bit of a problem.'

Dark eyes flashed. 'About Soph?' Leo pronounced it to rhyme with loaf. It was a habit of his to abbreviate any name that could be abbreviated, many that others thought could not. 'Soph's all right,' he added.

Ridiculously, Barbie was reassured. Leo had this effect on people.

'All the same,' she persevered. She had decided to consult Leo, and consult him she would.

Dark eyes crossed hers again, apparently read her mind. 'Come back for a bite,' he offered. A phrase he'd picked up from Lord Mummery originally, but that was now regarded as his own. Leo's bites, usually vast repasts in the somewhat sumptuous flat he inhabited round the corner from the hospital, were famous. He used them to transact business that, for one reason or another, could not easily be accommodated in the theatre, clinics or his own office. Leo's flat was almost an additional staff common room – and the food considerably better than the hospital provided. Only Leo himself knew that he filled the place deliberately.

For Leo had taken a hard knock when the girl he loved, who'd been on the professorial medical unit at the Central, had married someone else. He'd seen the inevitable coming towards him, had prepared himself for it, and – being both resilient and determined – he'd weathered the blow successfully. No one was more realistic than Leo. Nor was he a man to scorn second best. He was more than prepared to settle for friendship. But Jane was two hundred miles away, and these days he found the Central an empty place.

That evening he was glad to take Barbie home with him. He sat her down in a deep black leather chesterfield, buttoned and padded, gave her a brimming glass of gin and tonic, ice-cold, more gin than tonic. 'Though 'ow you can drink the vile stuff I don't comprehend,' he commented, pouring himself an equally generous whisky, collapsing with a grunt into his Charles Eames chair – black leather again, and rosewood, with a swivel base and its own leather footstool, on which he now stretched out a pair of neat little feet. 'Each to his own poison,' he added, downed a quantity of whisky. 'End of the day,' he announced. 'Thank Gawd for that. Started at 2.30 'smorning. 'Ad enough. Now, what's all this about Soph?'

Barbie told him.

'Pot?' he demanded. 'Nick Waring? Why wasn't I told? If it's true, that is.'

'Giles is sure of it.'

'Oh, 'im.' Leo had never been impressed by Giles Stanstead. ''As 'e told Steve King?' he asked sharply.

'No.' Barbie was sure of this.

''Oo 'as bin told?'

'Only you, now. We've kept it quiet. But I'm worried about Sophie.'

'So you said. Can't see why. Girl always keeps 'er 'ead.'

So Leo thought Sophie level-headed. He should know, if anyone, Barbie considered. She began to wonder if she was panicking about nothing. Perhaps Sophie was more than capable of running her own life? If Leo thought so, no doubt she was.

Leo did think so. But he was perturbed

about Nick. 'I suppose Stanstead is sure of 'is facts?' he demanded.

'He's smelt pot in that flat more than once. He's sure of that. Of course, it could be only Louise who smoked it, nothing to do with Nick. But if so, why did he go to pieces in that typical way?'

'By all accounts 'e went to pieces,' Leo agreed. 'I wasn't around at the time to form me own opinion, if you remember. I was in the States. It surprised me to 'ear it. I'd 'ave bet good money on Nick Waring ending up as R.S.O.'

'You thought he was as good as that?'

'Yeah. And 'e was as good as that, too. My opinion shared by others. Like Mummery, f'r instance. That laddie 'ad only to walk into the theatre, and 'e might 'ave been born and bred in it. 'E knew what was 'appening, 'e knew what was needed, most of the time 'e knew what to do about it. And 'e never panicked. Good anticipation, and a reliable grasp of detail.'

Barbie nodded. She had seen all this.

'They don't come like that often,' Leo reminded her. 'In fact, I was surprised young Waring came our way at all. Brilliant student. 'Ard working, too. Diagnostic flair. But I thought 'e was 'eading straight for the professorial medical unit. Quiet unassuming types like Waring usually make physicians, don't they? And undoubtedly the medical unit were sitting waiting for 'im. But 'e just sniffed the theatre, and there 'e stayed.'

Barbie remembered that, too. She nodded again, drank more gin, sighed.

'I thought 'e'd last the course,' Leo told her. 'I've seen a good many come and go, but you can normally tell in advance 'ow well they'll do. I never thought Waring'd break down. Not unless you came along and 'it 'im over the 'ead wiv an 'ammer, that's to say.'

'I'm sure he wouldn't have done if he hadn't had appalling bad luck. But it was Sophie I wanted to talk to you about, Leo. She seems to be rushing off to Eversholt's after him. And it's not her scene at all. She has no notion of what she may be letting herself in for.' As a staff nurse, Barbie had done her stint in Casualty. She thought she would remember for ever the young drug addicts brought in from Soho and the public lavatories in Leicester Square. They were filthy, most of their few belongings stolen as they lay in the streets. In Casualty, they'd been forced to set aside a room especially for them, warm and dry, but empty except for rubber mattresses. Here they could stay until they came round, when the police who had brought them in would very likely have to be called again to remove them, before they half-killed the staff or one another. The experience had scarred Barbie. Nowadays anything to do with drugs terrified her. 'Eversholt's, of all places,' she added despairingly. In her opinion, Eversholt's was a slum down by the shunting yards, under-staffed and dangerous, existing only to serve a population of layabouts, hooligans, meths drinkers, junkies and criminals. 'I can't bear to think of Sophie rambling round that area on her own.'

'Got 'er 'ead screwed on,' Leo reminded her, for the second occasion. 'Still, it is a bit off, I'll agree. I'll 'ave a word with the girl.'

He started as soon as he saw Sophie the following morning. 'What's all this about you going down to Eversholt's after young Waring?'

'Eversholt's? Nick?' Sophie was startled. 'Someone's been talking to you,' she said indignantly.

'Well, of course they 'ave. Otherwise I wouldn't know. Because you've said nothing.'

They looked accusingly at one another. Leo did not share the general opinion of

Sophie's fragility. Simply because the girl had small bones and big eyes, no reason to assume she was a tropical plant. Anyone who could stand the pace of working for him had to be tough, he made sure of that, and Sophie was the best secretary he'd ever had. What was more, she stood up to him, argued with him, bullied him into sitting down and answering his mail when he didn't feel in the least like it. By an inimitable blend of cajolery, mockery and downright defiance she sent him round the hospital to his myriad appointments punctually. She'd masterminded his trip to the U.S.A., too, fixed his travel out and back, booked his hotels and his hospital appointments, seen to it that he was free to concentrate on his lectures and demonstrations with no anxiety over the mechanics of daily living. On top of all that, she was running the General Surgical Unit's administration as it hadn't been run for years. Leo had no belief at all in her frailty. But he wanted to know what she was up to, wanted to hear more about young Nick, too. What had been happening while he was out of the country? It seemed he couldn't turn his back on the place for a month or two without a right old muddle.

'Has Giles been talking to you?' Sophie

was inquiring suspiciously.

'Nope. Barbie Henderson.' Leo could be relied on to produce straight answers to straight questions.

'Oh, I see. She and Giles both seem to think I ought to cut loose from Nick.'

Leo grinned. 'I can see why Giles would consider it an advantage, but you'll admit Bar may 'ave good reasons.'

'He's simply trying to cope with this sister on heroin.'

'On *heroin?*' No one had told Leo this. None of the consultants knew about it, other than the psychiatrist in charge of the drug application unit, and he'd kept his own counsel.

'Yes. When she arrived from Spain she was on heroin. That was the first problem. But Nick got treatment for her, and she's supposed to be cured.'

'For 'ow long?' Leo asked sceptically.

'Well, that's it, of course. That's what everyone wonders. Including Nick.'

'No wonder 'e got into several sorts of a stew. Poor young devil. 'Ow old is this sister of 'is?'

'She was seventeen when she arrived. She looks a good deal older, though. Very sophisticated, for one thing. A bit worn, too.

But she's the reason why he had to take this locum down at Eversholt's.'

'Why's that?'

'He had to have something quickly, and he wanted day duties only. He couldn't find a registrar's post where he could live out and have his evenings free, and of course there's this shortage of married quarters so no one would give him living-in accommodation for himself and his sister. After all, there are plenty of registrars with a wife and two kids who can't get married quarters, so what hope had he?'

'Does 'e 'ave to look after this blooming sister? Isn't there anyone else to take 'er on?'

'Only his mother, who's in Rome now. She's useless – more or less told Nick to get on with it.'

'I see.' He brooded. 'I'm sorry for young Nick,' he said finally. 'It's a poor outlook all round. But I'm sorry for you, too, Soph, if you let yourself get mixed up in that.'

'I must find out how he's getting on.'

''Aven't you heard, then?' Leo gave her a sharp appraising look.

Sophie flushed. 'No,' she said briefly.

'So what are you proposing to do?'

'I thought I'd go down and see him, perhaps,' Sophie admitted, cornered.

'Why use y'r legs? What's wrong with the telephone?'

'Too easy for him to put me off.'

'Stone the crows, Soph. Bar was right. You've got it bad.'

'All right then,' she blazed at him. 'So I've got it bad.' Green eyes flared across the desk. 'But I'm not going to let him drift out of my life because I'm too proud to chase after him, and find out how he is. At least I'll know I did what I could.'

This was the Sophie Leo recognized, and he knew she was unstoppable in that mood. 'Just take care then, duckie,' he said. 'Try not to get 'urt, won't you? More than you can 'elp, anyway.'

CHAPTER FOUR

CASUALTY OFFICER
AT EVERSHOLT'S

So now here she was, trudging along this seedy road, under the bridge, along by the marshalling yards. Goods trucks, piles of coke, the coal depot. A row of terraced houses, peeling stucco, cardboard notices in windows, corrugated iron blocking off gaping holes in brickwork, tattered posters flapping outside tiny neighbourhood shops. The saddest road in London, Leo had warned her. As usual he had been correct. Every house looked bug-ridden, greasy, squalid.

Sophie seemed to have been walking for a lifetime, lost in this grey limbo. Twelve minutes, she saw, checking her watch. Past the coal yard. An ambulance went by, turned in to the right. The hospital must at least exist, she thought, relieved. She had been beginning to imagine herself condemned for ever to walk down this derelict road to nowhere.

At last the hospital entrance. Looking like

any other hospital entrance. Railings, double gates, illuminated signs, a porter's lodge. Inside the lodge, no porter, but a middle-aged woman at a switchboard, knitting. 'Yes, dear?' Needles clicked indefatigably on.

'I was looking for Casualty.'

'Turn left and it's on the left.' The woman barely looked up, and Sophie left her counting stitches, walked on down the asphalt path past red brick walls and high windows with dirty frosted glass.

Eversholt's catered mainly now for the old and the chronic sick. Acute cases were admitted to the parent hospital in north London, Mortimer's. Eversholt's retained, though, the big out-patient department which had served the local population since the nineteen-thirties, when, formerly a work-house, it had been taken over by the London County Council under a new public health act. During the war the hospital had been bombed, and its buildings carried the marks still. Now it was scattered over its own spacious grounds between the railway and the coal depot, a conglomeration of lofty workhouse wards raised by the Victorians, more recent four-storey blocks put up by the L.C.C. and – most recent of all – prefabricated hutments, dotted about at random.

Sophie came to a parking space labelled 'Ambulances Only', occupied by a laundry van busily unloading. Swing doors with an illuminated sign 'Casualty'. She walked through, and inside the familiar hospital smell greeted her, together with the familiar sight of dark brown linoleum and dark brown tiles. A blaze of light, too, more frosted glass, reasonably clean here, though the cream paint on the walls showed a high-water mark seven feet from the ground, above which it became a very dark and dusty grey.

Five adults and two children were sitting on wooden benches while out of sight a great deal of door banging, running about and telephoning was going on. At a counter a good-looking Nigerian girl in a green overall was reading a magazine and stirring a cup of tea. She didn't raise her head.

Sophie, though, had been brought up in hospitals. She was accustomed to hunting her men through clinics and wards, and she proceeded to do this now. Looking over the tops of frosted glass panels, opening doors, casting the busy preoccupied look round that came naturally to her, and aroused no comment.

Inside the third door she came upon Nick. Tall, concentrated, frowning a little, he was examining a head wound. The patient was a curly-headed Irishman in overalls spattered with blood. 'Yes, well,' Nick was saying, 'I'll just put some stitches in this for you, you stay here and have a bit of a rest and a cup of tea, then you can go home and put your feet up. Where do you...' He looked up, saw Sophie. A light came on in his eyes, but all he said was 'Hullo, Soph.' He'd picked that up from Leo, sometimes used it as a joke. 'Where've you sprung from?' Suddenly he looked ten years younger, as if he hadn't a care in the world. 'Can you wait, say, ten minutes or quarter of an hour? I'll slip out for a word then.'

'Ten minutes, is it?' the patient demanded indignantly. 'Is that all the toime ye'll be after taking over me poor ould head, doctor?'

'Not much more,' Nick said absently, swabbing the wound, studying it. 'Perhaps twenty minutes before you're through. It's not as bad as it looks, you know. A lot of blood, but it's only a surface gash. You shouldn't even have a headache.'

'I'll wait,' Sophie said hastily.

Nick smiled at her. Sophie smiled back. Their smiles met and mingled, and even the preoccupied patient responded immediately.

'Hey, keep still,' Nick said sharply. 'I can't do this properly if you're going to jerk about like that. Sister...'

'It's just that I was allowing meself an eyeful of your bird, doctor, no more.' The patient was aggrieved. 'Sure, and ye'd niver be grudging me that pleasure, now, and me in me agony would ye?'

Nick grinned. He couldn't help it. He was one large grin, happiness was sparking out all over him. He was so filled with delight he thought he might very likely explode.

Sister Bowmaker thought so too. 'I've never seen a man change so,' she told her family that evening. She lived in one of the terrace houses in a little street just off the shunting yards. Her family had been there for more than a hundred years, and she had broken with tradition when she'd insisted on training at Eversholt's instead of marrying a railway-man and producing a brood of future rail-waymen. In due course she'd produced the brood all right, her husband a local green-grocer, and now, at fifty, a grandmother, she was back at Eversholt's, Casualty Sister from two till six, five days a week. A friend who'd trained with her did the morning shift. In many ways, Eversholt's was a local cottage hospital, staff and patients alike coming from

72

the wastelands between the railways. 'The moment this dizzy blonde walked through the door, Dr Waring lit up like a blooming Christmas tree. Did me good to see it. Nice to know there are still couples that can feel like that about each other.' She looked pointedly at her husband, who grunted, drank more tea. 'She felt it too, the blonde, no doubt of it,' Sister Bowmaker went on, her eyes soft with recollection. 'They stood there like a couple of kids, drinking each other in. But 'e went on and stitched the feller up as if 'e 'adn't another thought in 'is 'ead, I must say. Very neat with those long fingers of 'is, Dr Waring. And quick too. From the Central. They're good there, of course. 'E's a bit of a change, I can tell you, after that Dr Ebenezer we 'ad last. Slow as a month of Sundays, 'e was. 'Alf asleep most of the time, if you ask me. Drugged, some said. Proper dopey, 'e was. Now this Dr Waring, 'e's all of a jump. Where's this, what've you done about that, who's this, check the other. 'E keeps me on the 'op, I don't mind telling you. So I wasn't 'arf pleased to see this flash bird knock 'im all of a 'eap.'

The flash bird sat on one of the benches outside Nick's door, all of a heap herself.

This was Nick. She'd found him, and he

73

was exactly the same as he'd always been. Dear, familiar, beloved. Why had she been imagining he'd be in some way changed, simply because he'd left the Central? It was as if they'd met only yesterday, as if the past lonely month had never been. She and Nick were together again, and nothing else mattered. He'd been as pleased to see her as she had been to regain him, she knew that for sure. Soon he'd come to join her.

And then what?

Then they'd separate. He'd go back to his Louise, and she'd return to the Central and her job.

She shook her head. The future was nothing. Behind that door was Nick. She could see the shadow of his head as he moved.

Nick could catch sight of the top of Sophie's head as he finished stitching, gave the patient and Sister Bowmaker instructions. He began to wash his hands at the side basin, talking over his shoulder still to the relieved and now somewhat argumentative patient. But in his head a separate conversation was going on. 'Sophie's come,' his heart was shouting. 'Sophie's come. She's here.'

He ought to have known he could rely on her. Sophie wasn't a girl to forget. She simply came out to Eversholt's, hunted round.

Sophie was enduring. A girl you could rely on for ever. A fatuous grin curved his mouth, and the light behind his eyes refused to go out. He finished instructing Sister Bowmaker, dried his hands, put on his coat and walked out of the door to Sophie. Behind him, Sister Bowmaker and the patient crossed glances, and the patient winked. 'Got it bad, sister, has he not?'

Sister Bowmaker had her own thoughts, but she was not standing for any back chat about Dr Waring. 'It's you 'oo needed your 'ead examined, not 'im' she said tartly. 'Try keeping still for a change while I finish this off, if you don't mind.'

Nick walked straight over to the bench where Sophie sat. He took hold of both her hands, oblivious of the fascinated stare of the other occupants of the waiting hall, each of whom behaved as though they had been given special seats to observe a launch at Cape Kennedy. Sophie and Nick had forgotten the magnetism that flowed between them when they met after even a short absence, and they stood locked in sensation as the room shifted and the earth spun for them both. An electric current transfixed them, their hands were incapable of letting go. Both of them knew they were never going to let go again.

They spoke abruptly, at the same moment.

'I was wondering if...'

'How much time have...'

Silence fell. The waiting patients shifted, enthralled. A telephone shrilled, a door banged.

'Are you doing anything this evening, Sophie?' Nick asked.

'No. Not unless...'

'Will you come and have a meal?'

Sophie nodded. She noticed she was still clutching Nick's hands, loosened her hold, then smoothed his fingers, curved her own round them. Somehow they seemed to be clasping both hands together as tightly as before. 'Nick, I...'

'I'll clear up a bit here, see to one or two oddments. Will you wait?'

She nodded. This time they succeeded in releasing one another, Nick walked briskly back to join Sister Bowmaker and the Irish-man, while Sophie sat down on the bench again. Something odd in the air percolated through her daze, and she looked round.

Seven pairs of eyes were glued to her.

Or eight, to be precise. The Nigerian girl closed her magazine, walked over to her. 'If you're going to hang on for Dr Waring,' she said companionably, 'you can borrow my book. I've got my floors to finish. You can leave it on the table when you go.'

'Thank you very much.'

'My pleasure. Your coat's fab, if you don't mind me saying. Should turn him on for sure.' White teeth flashed, brown eyes brimmed with encouragement before, her blow struck for the female trade union, she disappeared down the corridor, where she could be heard singing to the accompaniment of considerable banging and knocking.

Sophie thankfully hid her face, and the fatuous smile that would keep returning to it, in the magazine.

Half an hour later, she and Nick were walking along the asphalt drive together, past the porter's lodge, and through the big gates. The switchboard operator looked up from her knitting this time, riveted. Knitting forgotten, she turned to her board, manipulated switches. 'Cas? That you, Mrs B? I say your new young man's just walked out with a smashing blonde.'

Eversholt's might be down in the wasteland between the railways, its medical and surgical standards might not be those of a top London teaching hospital, but its grapevine was outclassed by none. Its feminine intuition rated highly too. Nick's first words, as they left the hospital and began walking along the squalid road, would have pleased the Nigerian orderly. He held Sophie's hand, swung it gently looked at her suede jacket with its fur collar and cuffs, and remarked. 'That's a super coat, Sophie. You look terrific in it.'

Sophie looked slantwise back at him. 'I'm glad you like it. I wondered if you would, when I bought it.'

'Oh, God, Sophie. You shouldn't be going around buying coats and thinking about me.' The words were genuine, but his lips smiling down at her gave them the lie.

'Why not?' Sophie demanded, smiling back.

'I've muddled my life up hopelessly, and there's Louise. I'm no good to you.'

Sophie asked what seemed to her the logical question. 'How *is* Louise?'

'I wish I knew.' Now he did sound depressed. 'Oh, she's all right, I suppose. Don't let's talk about her,' he added. 'I have enough of her, without wasting this lovely evening.'

The evening was dreary. Misty and damp, the pavement greasy and filthy under their feet, the noise of heavy lorries and railway coaches thundered and clattered in their ears, drowning their conversation, while the smell of coal dust and diesel fumes mingled pungently with fish and chips. Frying tonight, as it didn't need the placard to announce. In the dusk, Nick took Sophie's hand again, looked down at her sleek head poised above the soft fur collar. The pale sensitive features that he knew so well, and loved so much, looked up at him in the way he was never able to forget, though he'd tried hard enough.

'What would you like to do?' he asked vaguely.

Sophie shrugged narrow shoulders. 'Anything. It doesn't matter. Go back to your flat and cook ourselves a meal?'

'No.' It was an explosion. 'Not there.'

'All right,' Sophie agreed equably. 'Not there, then.'

'It's just…' he began. Then shrugged in his turn. 'Oh, forget it.' He put his arm round her, she leant her head against his shoulder. Their steps matching, slowly and dreamily they emerged on to the busy Euston Road, crossed over, wandered on along South-ampton Row.

'I don't know where we're going,' Nick said suddenly. 'There's too much traffic noise to hear ourselves, too. Why don't we turn off?'

'Let's.'

They found themselves in a tiny oasis between the hurtling traffic and the towering office blocks. Narrow and charming, bow-windowed eighteen-century terraces linked Southampton Row with yet another wasteland of garages and factory space. Two young Londoners, one tall and dark, the other small and blonde, they strolled on together, bemused, came on a quiet crescent of Regency houses round a garden with tennis courts, overshadowed by huge office blocks, surrounded by acres of new council flats of glass and concrete. Then they came to Coram Fields, the original site of the Foundling Hospital, and nearby the Institute of Child Health. They crossed into Lamb's Conduit Street, a village shopping centre in the heart of the capital, and went into the pub there where Nick had often been as a student after lectures at the Institute. They found a small table tucked away in the corner, Sophie hung her suede jacket over the back of her chair, pushed her hair out of her eyes, and smiled at Nick.

He smiled back. 'Would you rather go to a show, or a film?' he asked conscientiously.

'Couldn't we just talk?'

His face lit up in that way it had, that she remembered so well, had missed so much. 'Of course,' he said. He took her hand, laid it against his cheek. 'Oh, love, I've missed you.'

'I've missed you,' she said softly. Her love for him warmed him through to his bones, offered a safe haven for ever.

'Oh Nick, I wish you hadn't left the Central,' she exclaimed sadly. 'When does your post at Eversholt's finish?' This, after all, was what she had come to find out.

'They've asked me to stay on for another month.'

'And you will?'

'Another month'll be useful. Give me a chance to look round, make up my mind.'

'Make up your mind about what?'

'About staying in London, or moving out into the provinces. And if so, whereabouts.'

'Oh,' Sophie said blankly. 'Yes, I see.'

'There's no particular point that I can see in staying in London if I can't get a job at the Central. More sensible to move out. There's more choice.'

'Yes. Yes, of course, there must be.' Desolation drowned her.

'The trouble is Louise. She doesn't want

81

to leave London.'

'So what?' Sophie demanded irritably.

He shook his head. 'She's not fit to look after herself,' he pointed out.

'Then it's about time she learnt.'

He sighed. 'Yes, well,' he said. 'Let's not bother with her now. I spend enough time thinking about her.' He took Sophie's hand again, began bending her fingers this way and that. 'Let's at least forget Louise for this evening. How's everyone at the Central? Tell me the latest. How's Giles getting on?'

Sophie didn't feel up to talking about how Giles was doing in the job with Stephen King. So she began instead to talk about the flat. 'You know he took over your flat – well, he's painted it navy blue and emerald green everywhere.' She remembered Giles asserting that Nick smoked pot, how angry she'd felt. This made something else not to pass on to Nick, and as she rejected it, she heard herself babbling on, describing the chrome settee and chairs, the glass-topped coffee tables. But this too was the wrong subject to choose.

'Clearly very trendy and affluent,' Nick commented caustically. 'A suitable pad for a rising young registrar.' From the beginning he'd felt badly about the Chalk Farm flat.

Now he felt worse. He thought with hatred of Giles, doing his job, working in the Central's theatres for Stephen King, living in his flat, painting it up, inviting Sophie to sit on a chrome chair, drink coffee at a glass-topped table. Sophie and Giles. Only to be expected of course. And he had no right to step between them, to try and get her back. A flood tide of jealousy submerged him. Despair ate into him. All he wanted was to get away, to prevent Sophie from finding out how much this mattered to him. Abruptly he pushed his chair back. 'Another drink?' he asked. 'Or shall we go and find that steak house?'

The evening disintegrated. They found the steak house, had rump steak with mushrooms and tomatoes, a bottle of wine. They might have been eating cardboard.

After the meal they separated politely. Sophie would not allow Nick to see her home, so much out of his way, she said. He made no attempt to persuade her. Momentarily they clung together in unacknowledged anguish, then wrenched themselves free, set off hastily in opposite directions.

As he reached the corner Nick turned, saw Sophie's slim back whisking round the end of the road. For a second he stopped dead, almost swung round to follow her, catch her up, tell her he couldn't bear to lose her. Instead he shook his head, strode decisively northwards towards Chalk Farm.

Sophie, too, had nearly turned round. But not quite. She joined a queue, waited for a bus, stared miserably into the night. What had gone wrong? The evening that had opened in such joyous certainty had ended only in this bleak separation.

Back in St Anne's Square, she climbed steadily up to her own flat. Under the telephone on the hall table was a note from Barbie, a telephone message.

For a moment of blinding joy she was certain Nick must have called her already. She grabbed the piece of paper. In Barbie's hasty scrawl, it stated. 'Giles rang. Several times. Says will you ring him back whatever time you get in.'

She picked up the telephone.

CHAPTER FIVE

NICK AND LOUISE

Nick swung northwards up Southampton Row, busy at this hour with late buses, newspaper vans racing to the railway stations with the next morning's papers, vegetable lorries thundering to market. He hated the battering noise, but he hated his own thoughts more, and knew better than to attempt to seek the peace of the quiet byways he had explored earlier with Sophie. They'd hold no peace for him now. Only angry, useless regret. He'd lost Sophie to Giles.

Crossing the Euston Road, he walked sadly on past Eversholt's until he reached the drab flat in Chalk Farm. Louise was in, her belongings scattered everywhere. Shoes on the shabby hearthrug, bag spilling open on the sofa, her coat there too. Her long silk scarf on the kitchen door, an apple browning on the mantelpiece. Cigarette stubs and ash everywhere. Unwashed plates and mugs on the kitchen table, with congealed potato salad and some sort of sausage.

He swore. Surely he was at least capable of seeing that they didn't live like this?

The following day, though, he awoke filled with surging energy. He was going to need it. That evening, when he returned from Eversholt's about half past six, Louise was lying on the sofa, in her dirty old housecoat, languid and bleary-eyed. He had been shopping, was carrying a big carton from the dairy. Fresh bread, butter, bacon, eggs, cheese. He looked at her sharply. 'Haven't you been up all day, Lulu?'

'Not really,' she admitted, yawning. 'I had a bath earlier, and a sort of a meal. Good thing you've done some shopping. There doesn't seem to be anything left.'

Nick dumped the carton down on the kitchen table, slammed the door on the room littered with dirty crockery, damp towels from the bathroom draped over the gas stove. 'We can't go on like this,' he said furiously.

'Oh, Nickie.' A pathetic wail. 'Don't say you've come back in a temper? And I was so looking forward to when you'd get in and talk to me.' She was injured, hard-done-by.

'This is serious, Lulu,' he said. 'I mean it. We must do some sensible planning. I'm going to look for a permanent post. You realize it won't necessarily be here in London?'

'Not in London?' She gaped at him. 'But what about me?'

'That's what we have to talk about.' He took a deep breath, prayed for strength. 'You can either find a job of some sort or do a training. I'll pay for that, if you promise to stick to it. Or, of course, you can come with me wherever I find a post. But in the long run you must do some work. You can't go on like this.'

'How can I?' She was flabbergasted, stared at him. 'I can't possibly. I've never had to do a *job*.'

She sounded like Marie Antoinette, he thought, or the Tsarina before the revolution. 'You must find something definite to do all day. Not drift on like this.'

'Oh,' she squeaked, hit the sofa cushions in her annoyance, 'oh, it's ridiculous. All this simply because you come in and I don't happen to be dressed. So we must turn our lives upside down.'

'You ought to have some sort of regular routine.'

'What for, for heaven's sake? What would be the point? Anyone would think routine was the answer to all life's problems.'

'It does you no good to be lying about all day with nothing to do.' Even to himself he sounded like a gramophone record of great grandmamma.

'What am I supposed to do with myself, day after day, in this ghastly place, tell me that,' she challenged him.

Tempted to say 'You could try cleaning the place up, getting in some food,' he bit the words back. No use breaking off for a quarrel about who did what.

'You're so neat and meticulous,' Louise stated accusingly, rather as though these qualities were deadly sins. 'Do you ever stop to think of the hours you waste, fussing away in your tidy little antiseptic shell, while life passes you by?'

Eversholt's, he longed to retort, far from being the antiseptic shell she evidently imagined, a refuge from all demands, was in fact a crude, messy sort of human workroom, where life in the raw was apt to present itself hourly. 'It's not exactly like that,' he commented dryly.

Louise, well into her stride by now, ignored him. 'Stuck in your nine to six rut in your grotty old job,' she declaimed, 'you don't know what it is to *live*. Your sort of existence would never do for me. I've been brought up in a sunny country, by the Mediterranean. Mountains, vineyards, wine and olives and...' she paused momentarily for inspiration, rapidly got steam up again '...dancing all night, meeting people who know how to enjoy themselves, people with money, town houses and country houses. Yachts, cars, servants to see to everything, lovely couture clothes and parties all the time. Every day.'

Her eyes, he saw with a pang of irritated affection, were nostalgic, as she dwelt on these past glories. She was pathetic, and he felt very angry with Trish, taking her up and dropping her as the mood took her, failing even to support her financially.

'And now,' Louise turned on him angrily, 'now, as if it isn't bad enough in this awful flat in this fearful weather, you expect me to get a job as well. Go out and wait in the freezing cold in the rush hour for buses that never come.'

'Other people do,' he said shortly, exasperated.

She began to wheedle. 'I don't want to leave London, Nickie. If I've got to live in this dismal country – and I suppose I have – at least let it be in London, where there's something going on.' Unexpectedly she began to cry. 'You only want to get rid of me,' she gulped. 'You're like everyone else in the end. People always go off me, only I thought you were different. But now you have too. Nobody ever wants me for long.'

She was right, of course. He was fed up to the teeth with having her around. He had never meant her to find out, though. What was he to do now? Hands jammed in his pockets, he frowned at the floor. He was at a standstill. But he had to say something. 'Look, Lulu,' he began gently. 'You don't have to rush off and find a job if it honestly seems so awful. But suppose I stayed in London, would you find an occupation that interested you, something to do every day? A course of study, perhaps – a language, say, Italian, or Spanish?' he suggested vaguely, floundering.

'I can speak Spanish fluently, thank you,' she said snappishly. However, she brightened up at the prospect of remaining safely in London with him. 'I'll tell you what, how would it be if I took up my painting again?'

He was cautious. 'Your painting, Lulu? I...'

'I've been slack about it lately, I know. There was so little time in Spain, I rather let it go. But a lot of people say I'm really quite good. I'll start again shall I? I could enrol at that place in Holborn, perhaps, if you think I ought to go to some classes. Peregrine knows all about it, I'll ask him.' The crisis past, she smiled brilliantly. 'By the way, he says he'll have an assignment for me next week. Down on the coast somewhere. Hampshire, I believe he said.'

'What sort of assignment?'

'Oh, fashions, I think.' She was airy. 'Some colour supplement feature on cotton for the middle of next summer, no doubt. He said we'd probably be away four or five days, in any case. So I won't be getting under your feet for a bit, and there should be loads of lovely bread too.'

The week without her was comfortable and easy. Nick enjoyed it. He was able to leave in time each morning for Eversholt's, come back to a quiet evening's uninterrupted reading. He was soon wondering whether he should ring Sophie, see how she was.

Throughout the following day, in every gap between patients, his hand stretched hopefully towards the telephone. Finally he gave in, rang her. He knew at once he'd made the right decision. Simply to hear Sophie's voice restored his faith in himself. 'How are you, Sophie?'

'I'm fine, Nick. How are you?'

'Oh, I'm fine. How's life?'

'Not bad at all. How are you doing?'

'Might be worse.'

Hardly scintillating conversation. But it filled him with delight and happiness. He had meant only to find out how she was, but he seemed now to have said something about a meal, to have asked her to meet him. Sophie reciprocated with tickets for the Royal Festival Hall. She had two for the Beethoven concert that Leo had passed on to her, as he had to go out of London to see a patient.

They arranged to meet in Lamb's Conduit street again, have a snack, walk through Gray's Inn and Lincoln's Inn to the riverside, and then the South Bank. Nick put down the telephone, grinned broadly at an astonished builder's labourer who had come in to have his stitches out. He continued to grin most of the afternoon and Sister Bowmaker was forced to inquire from the switchboard who it was that Dr Waring had rung at tea time. 'Because I wondered if it was that blonde,' she suggested. 'He's been like a cat with two tails ever since.'

'If her name is Sophie, it was, and she's at the Central,' responded the chief of intelligence at Eversholt's briskly. 'Mr Rosenstein's secretary, 'e asked for, "'ullo, Sophie," 'e said.'

The intelligence network at the Central was also busy. There they had been watching, fascinated, Giles's pursuit of Sophie. On the whole they approved. Few people failed to respond to Giles – though one of these was Leo Rosenstein, who informed his theatre sister that he was sorry to hear of the new set-up. Sophie had been far better off with Nick Waring, in his opinion. Worth two of Giles Stanstead any day.

'She's going out with Nick again tomorrow, you know,' Barbie sighed. 'Apparently you've given her tickets for a concert, and she's taking Nick to it.' She regarded Leo accusingly.

'I gave 'er no instructions about 'oo she was to take with 'er, Bar. Be y'r age. 'Ow could I?'

'Well, I wish she'd stop seeing him. Only misery can come of it.'

But Nick and Sophie, unaware of anything remotely like impending misery, passed a magic evening, marred only by the necessity for it to come to an end.

The moment Sophie had come through the door, Nick knew beyond doubt that they were meant to spend their lives together, that the days in St Anne's Square had marked the beginning of two shared lives. Abruptly he reached a decision. He was going to get Sophie away from Giles. She belonged to him. As Beethoven thundered majestically over them, he held her hand securely in his own, longed to remain holding it for ever. First of all, though, he'd have to organize a life for himself and Louise that Sophie could reasonably be asked to share. It would take time – and determination – but he'd damn well do it. Could he expect Sophie to be available still, when at length he achieved it? He reckoned he could.

Even so, when he returned to the squalid flat and Louise, he was more desolate than he would have believed possible.

Unexpectedly, however, life took a turn for the better. Louise came back from her travels in Hampshire saying she'd probably found a job. 'Peregrine says you're quite right,' she informed the startled Nick. 'He agrees I ought to have a job and a regular routine, just what you said.' She pulled a face. 'He's taking me out this evening to meet Willie Hampson. He runs an antique shop in Hampstead, and he's looking for an assistant, Peregrine says.'

Nick, whose jaw had dropped, closed his mouth, swallowed, still found nothing to say.

His mind buzzed. Was this some ploy of Peregrine's? Who was this convenient antique-shop owner? Why did he suddenly need an assistant? And given that his need might be genuine, why Louise?

He told himself not to be so sceptical and suspicious. After all, Louise could be both decorative and charming. Not everyone knew the Louise he saw at home. So quite likely this man Willie Hampson might take her on. How long, though, would she last? Even Peregrine must know that Louise was hardly likely to hold the job down for more than a few weeks.

Blithely, Louise departed for the meeting. She was back, bubbling with delight, radiant, at two in the morning, woke Nick to tell him she'd landed the job. 'I start tomorrow,' she said. 'From ten to six every day, and I have my lunch in Willie's flat above the shop. He says his housekeeper is a very good cook. Work all day Saturday, Sunday and Monday off. So you were quite right to tell me to settle down and find a job. I'm sorry I was so cross about it at the time. Look what it's led to. From now on I shall be a reformed character. You'll see. Earning good money, too. The only snag is, you'll have to dig me out every morning. I'll never be able to get myself up.'

Dig her out every morning he did. It was a struggle for both of them, but he gathered it worked, that she succeeded in arriving at the shop in Hampstead in reasonable time each day. Often she didn't return until late in the evening, but when she came in she was usually able to give him a coherent account of where she had been and what she had done. Sometimes, as so often, out with Peregrine to meet 'useful people', sometimes in the shop with Willie, cataloguing, and then eating dinner in the flat upstairs – Willie's housekeeper, she said, was indeed a superb cook, as he had told her, and she was always quick to snap up any invitation to stay on and eat there.

As far as Nick could make out, Louise was telling him the truth. He could relax, assume that at least temporarily she was settled in good hands, turn his mind to his post at Eversholt's. Here he was unmistakably doing well. He was the best Casualty Officer they'd had for a long while, and they determined to hang on to him.

Eversholt's future was uncertain, had been for more than ten years, and this made staffing the hospital an even bigger headache than usual. The parent hospital, Mortimer's

Infirmary, a series of huge red brick Victorian blocks on the slopes where Hampstead merged into Kilburn, wanted to move Eversholt's patients to the main hospital, building new wards to house them. The Department of Health, recognizing that if the Eversholt's site was abandoned, valuable land would be available for sale in central London, had agreed to this. The Department applied for planning permission, in order to sell the site for office development, and promised Mortimer's a substantial slice from the proceeds.

However, at this stage the government fell, and the plan became so much waste paper, the incoming government opting for a comprehensive school on the site. Eversholt's was to be closed immediately under this scheme, patients transferred to different hospitals throughout the region. The news leaked out. There was an outcry, tremendous local indignation, a campaign in the press. Casualty, the first department to close, had to be hurriedly reopened, staff at first sent down in buses from Mortimer's itself, and Patrick Croham, their senior orthopaedic surgeon, once more found himself saddled with Eversholt's Casualty Department. He protested furiously, fought numerous battles in committee. 'It's not safe,' he reiterated constantly. 'We can't cover it adequately. The other day in the rush hour it took me over forty minutes to get there. A patient will die. There'll be an emergency, and we'll be too far away to deal with it. You can't expect a mixed bunch of junior residents, half of them unable to communicate with each other because of language difference, to throw up someone capable of initiating prompt action on the spot. In my opinion, we shouldn't touch the place with a barge pole. Let some hospital near by provide consultant cover. The Central's just round the corner – let them take it on.' But Mortimer's were not prepared to hand any part of Eversholt's over to the Central. They needed the beds for their chronic cases, and they intended to collect the money that would eventually accrue from the sale of the site. No other London hospital was going to scoop up that prize. 'I know, old boy, Eversholt's may not be instantly recognizable as a prize of any sort – least of all to you,' the chairman of the medical committee commiserated with Croham, 'but we can't afford to wave it good-bye, can we? We'll be waving good-bye to a million or two at the same time.'

Before he'd been finally overruled, however, Croham had succeeded in reaching a minor compromise. Casualty at Eversholt's would be open only from nine to six daily. After that, emergencies would be routed to the Central London Hospital.

Croham continued to complain. 'The whole set-up is dominated by politics,' he pointed out to anyone prepared to listen. 'Medical needs are being entirely ignored. They count for nothing. Closing the hospital down to build a school was a political decision. Then when the public made a fuss, the politicians saw they might lose a few votes, so they did a quick about-turn, and the place had to be opened again. None of that has anything to do with the care of the patient. And now we're playing the same game ourselves – hanging on to it simply because we're dead scared that if the Central get their hands on one run-down hospital on their doorstep, which they're far more capable of staffing than we are, they're going to end up sitting on the cash that we want for our new buildings. As a result I'm landed with responsibility for a casualty department that ought to have stayed closed.' The department gave him recurrent nightmares. But now, with Nick's appointment, everything changed. 'The entire department has a different atmosphere,' Croham informed the senior orthopaedic registrar at Mortimer's, one day when they were gossiping over a cup of tea after his list. 'Waring has them all running round like scalded cats.' He chuckled, drank more tea. 'They seem quite energetic and lively down there these days, instead of ambling about asleep on their feet. It's the same staff, so how he's achieved it I can't imagine. Why the Central let him go is a mystery to me, too. I thought at first he simply had a month or two to fill in between posts, but yesterday when he called me out to see a patient, I took the opportunity to ask him about his next post. He muttered something about having to see what he could get, perhaps he'd go outside London, he wasn't sure. So I take it the Central don't want him.'

'Or not yet, at any rate. He may be waiting for a specific job.'

'I don't think he'd consider leaving London if he was doing that. He'd want to be seen around the place from time to time. Wouldn't you?'

His senior registrar grinned broadly, agreed. 'Very much so. You're right, sir. Out of sight, out of mind.'

'That's how it's apt to go, I'm afraid. So we can assume the Central are through with him. I haven't met anyone who knows why, but then I don't know many Central people. However, their loss is our gain. I'm going to hang on to him. At least with him, we're in no danger of another episode like that affair of the blood transfusion last year. I still wake up in a sweat over that. The patient would have died, you know, if I hadn't happened to be in the building.'

This narrow escape had occurred during the first week of a new appointment. The new Casualty Officer came from a medical family of high standing in his own country, but no one knew until too late that he was regarded with deep scorn by his more competent relatives, who had worked with united fervour to push him through medical school, had then thankfully washed their hands of him. He'd come to England to escape them all, and, with the right examinations behind him, excellent references from his father's friends, and a polished manner often lacking in junior staff, he'd had no difficulty in finding a post.

During his second day at Eversholt's, there had been a minor accident on the railway. One of the linesmen had been injured by a shunting train.

Patrick Croham was about to begin his

ward round in the main block, when the new Casualty Officer had rung him, told him of the admission. 'Multiple injuries to both lower limbs,' he reported.

'I see,' Croham said. 'Well, get some blood into him, clean him up and so on, and I'll come in and have a look at him after my round. All right?'

'Yes, sir. Thank you,' the Casualty Officer said politely. He hadn't the faintest idea how to get some blood into the man. It was a procedure he'd never been asked to carry out at home. In a panic – which his family would have spotted at once, but which no one at Eversholt's diagnosed – he told Sister Bowmaker to get the man cleaned up.

After this, no one could find him, until eventually the switchboard tracked him down in his bedroom. 'Yes, yes,' he said irritably. Tell sister he was on his way back.

However, he failed to appear. Sister Bowmaker rang his room. He was irritable at being rung a second time. 'I told them I'd be over, sister.'

'I don't like the look of the patient,' Sister Bowmaker said. 'I'd like you to come and examine him as soon as possible. I think he needs some blood.'

'We can discuss that when I examine him,'

the young man said hurriedly, rang off, returned to his textbooks. He knew the theory of giving blood all right. It was the practicalities that escaped him. In any case, he hoped a little procrastination would save him from making a fool of himself in his new hospital. If he hung about long enough, someone else would have done the job before his return. In the past he had always found this method most effective.

He had not, however, dealt with Sister Bowmaker in the past. Increasingly anxious about the patient, she ignored protocol, had Mr Croham called out of his ward round to the telephone, though even in Eversholt's this was seldom done 'Worried, are you, sister?' he asked. 'How much blood has he had?'

The answer, of course, was none.

Patrick Croham left his registrar to complete the round, came across to Casualty at the gallop with the orthopaedic housemen panting alongside. He spent an hour and a half on the patient. Calm, matter-of-fact, placid. The Casualty Officer, strolling in half-way through, thought he'd got away with it. Afterwards, though, Croham turned to him. 'A word with you – sister, might I borrow your office for a few minutes? Thank you so much.'

No one knew what he'd said. But that particular Casualty Officer had gone at the end of the week, and until his chastened departure one of the orthopaedic registrars from Mortimer's had remained immovably in the department.

Since then Eversholt's had had a succession of Casualty Officers. A few good, most indifferent, some downright hopeless. Nick stood head and shoulders above the lot of them, and, to no one's surprise except his own, was offered the post for the next six months.

He accepted at once. It was amazingly reassuring to be offered a job. Having to leave the Central had demoralized him. Failure there, coupled with his inability to deal with Louise, had demolished his confidence.

The extra money would be useful, too. The horrible flat was not cheap. Nowhere in London was cheap these days, and this slum took half his salary after tax. Even this disadvantage, though, was to be remedied. Sister Bowmaker offered him the unfurnished flat in her basement. This was Eversholt's version of subsidized accommodation, though the subsidy came from the Bowmakers' own pockets. Partly from genuine kindness, and partly because it suited them to have junior hospital doctors in their basement, they offered the flat at a low rent. One of the Indian registrars had been living there with his wife and baby for the past two years, but he was going home now to practise.

The flat was not grand, Sister Bowmaker said apologetically, but if he'd like to look at it he was welcome. It had been occupied by her husband and herself when they first married, she told him, and they'd done it up then. When her Dad died, though, they'd moved upstairs with her Mum. 'It's clean and dry. You provide your own furniture – you did say you'd got some in store didn't you?'

There was nothing, he suspected, that Sister Bowmaker didn't know about his life and background. He grinned cheerfully at her, agreed that he had furniture in store, fixed an evening to see the flat. When he saw it, he took it. It was a great deal cheaper than his present flat, cleaner too, and there was a coal fire in the living room. He liked that. 'Like home,' he said to Louise. 'Sitting in front of our own fire again. Of course, it's a terrible road, but once inside it's not half bad, you'll find.'

She looked uneasy, faintly guilty.

He knew that look so well. What was she up to now?

'It can hardly be worse than this place, can it?' she asked. 'This is a slum. And now a basement in what you say yourself is a terrible road. You've got a nerve, Nickie, the places you expect me to live in.'

If she had not landed on him with all her problems, he would have been at the Central still, he thought, living in the St Anne's Square flat, with Sophie upstairs. He set his lips, to prevent hot phrases of recrimination from pouring destructively out.

But when she wanted to, Louise could read him as clearly as he read her. 'You've gone off me, Nickie,' she said sadly. 'People always get tired of me, want to be rid of me. You pretend not to be like that, but you are. It's only duty that makes you put up with me at all.'

The second time she had accused him of this. And it was the truth, at least partly. This was where he failed her. He could provide a roof over her head, but he couldn't give her what she most longed for, a sense of being needed and wanted. But it wasn't the whole truth. More than duty kept them together. He loved her. But did she love him – or anyone?

'You'd heave a sigh of relief,' she was saying, 'if someone took me off your hands.'

Her own attitude was so plainly the source of her trouble that Nick was unable to keep his mouth shut any longer. 'Just like you, Lulu,' he heard himself retort. 'But why should anyone have to take you off my hands. Why can't you try to stand on your own two feet, run your own life? All these moans about people not wanting you. What about you wanting them? Do you want me? Like hell you do. You want a meal ticket and a roof over your head. That's all. But you're a big girl now, love. Grown up. Remember?'

'Oh, thanks very much,' she said resentfully. 'The order of the boot. Well, as it happens I'm already fixed up. I was going to tell you anyway. I'm not going to live here or anywhere else with you any longer. No more slumming for me. I'm moving into Willie's flat permanently. He's asked me to, and I said I would, so there.'

'*Willie?*'

'Willie.' She was triumphant. 'It's a super flat. Central heating, too, and loads of hot water. And a housekeeper to see to the food. No need to look like that, either. I know he's old enough to be my father. It's simply a business arrangement, and I'll be living above the shop. Exactly the sort of routine you're always recommending.'

Nick pulled himself together. 'You don't have to do this, you know, Lulu. You can come and try the new flat with me.'

She shook her head. 'No, thanks. Hampstead is much nicer than King's Cross, for one thing. And after all, I'm only doing exactly what you said I ought to do, standing on my own feet, making a life for myself. So I don't see why you have to make difficulties. Peregrine thinks it's a splendid idea. Of course, Willie is a funny old thing, I know. But I like him. And he is like a father.'

This gave Nick the clue that he had up to now missed: Louise wanted a father, always had done, and now Willie Hampson was to be fitted into the role. Nick sighed, hoped her disillusionment would not be too abrupt. At least he could make it easy for her to return. 'Come and see the new flat, anyway, Lulu,' he urged her. 'You can tell me where to put the furniture and so on.' Instead of Sophie, he thought regretfully. For one carefree moment he'd imagined himself shedding Louise and her problems, calling in Sophie with a clear conscience. Asking her to help him establish himself in a flat which would be a haven for the two of them, as St Anne's

Square had once been. Now he pushed this dream resolutely to one side. Louise's father-figures were passing fantasies, only. But he was genuinely her brother. She was part of his childhood, and he couldn't' shrug her off, forget her, if he tried. What was more, deep down she knew this, counted on it, whatever she might say in the heat of the moment. For Louise he would always have to be on call.

CHAPTER SIX

THE FLAT IN MINSTER ROW

On Saturday, Peregrine came in his Citroën Safari to move Louise and her luggage to Hampstead. Gay, excited, more cheerful than Nick had seen her for weeks, she kissed him fervently, clung to him lovingly, pressed her address and telephone number on him. 'Come and see me, Nickie, as soon as you're settled.'

'Come on, Lulu, hurry up,' Peregrine, in a white leather coat lined with sheepskin, presumably selected to match his white Citröen, hustled her out. 'I haven't got all day, you know. I must be over the other side of London before two. Don't stand about, dear.' Vibrating with tension, he flicked ash while his eyes darted round the room.

Obediently, Louise hugged Nick again, dashed down the stairs, pursued by Peregrine. Nick looked round the shattered room. It had been a ruin when they first entered it, and it remained one. Stripped of their possessions, it had reverted to its own tawdry shabbiness. A seedy flat in a squalid street. He hoped never to set eyes on it again, was thankful to be leaving.

Sister Bowmaker's husband turned up in his greengrocery van and collected him. Nick piled in his cases, the cardboard boxes of books and groceries, and they were off.

Down by the railway the afternoon was cold and misty, but Sister Bowmaker had lighted a fire in the front room, flames flickered on walls that the Indians had painted apricot. The furniture had arrived the previous day. He set his roll-top desk in the corner, the Welsh dresser alongside the fireplace for books, the gateleg table in the window. Traffic thundered by, trains jolted over points, shunted. Upstairs, where three generations of Bowmakers lived, there were two radios and the television on the go, a baby crying lustily, a washing machine and a Hoover. He didn't mind any of it. He was at home by his own fireside, the family possessions around him. Life was looking up. He could call his soul his own again.

He made himself a cup of tea, sat down by the flickering flames to drink it, his feet on the long-haired modern rug that he had bought hurriedly, when he had had to replace his yellow Afghan. One day when he was at hospital, Louise had sold this. The memory of the row they had had as a result could still make him shiver. The episode marked one of his most depressing failures.

He had handled the affair badly from beginning to end, he could see that now. When he arrived home, he had been amazed to find the rug gone, had wandered at first, puzzled and at a loss, through the flat. Could Louise have taken it to be cleaned? He could hardly imagine anything more unlikely. The suspicion that she had sold it to provide herself with ready cash had seeped uneasily into his consciousness. At first he rejected it. But he began to remember how, as a child, she had been given to small acts of pilfering at intervals. Pocket money, the cash for the milk bill, odd scarves, little pottery ornaments. The Afghan rug, though, was valuable. His only valuable possession, in fact. Could they have been burgled? Was he doing Louise an injustice? He went through the flat again, checking. Nothing else was missing, but in her wardrobe hung a new maxi-coat and a pair of thigh boots he'd not seen before, and later, when she came in, he saw she was wearing tapestry trousers, the latest craze, with a sort of tabard to match, and a toning mohair sweater with a huge rolled collar.

A complete new outfit, from his Afghan rug. He had lashed out, vehement because, in one sense, while outraged, he'd been thankful too. The money had not been taken for drugs. Only for clothes. And like an angry parent whose child escapes death, he had attacked her with a furious tongue.

She had responded in kind, of course. And since her tongue was far less inhibited than his, he had very much the worst of the encounter.

Louise, as far as he could tell, remained offended with him, but delighted with her purchases, considering – unlike him – that she had achieved a good bargain. 'Such a fuss, Nickie, about a thoroughly dreary old rug. Just the sort of object you would want to clutter the place up with. We're much better off without it,' she commented airily.

Worse was to come. Still dazed, uncertain how to deal with Louise, he had heard a knock on the door, had known it must be Sophie. In his clumsy embarrassment, he had gone out to speak to her on the landing, holding the flat door closed behind him so that she should not see into the denuded room with its bare floor. It was Sophie who had chosen the yellow curtains to pick up the colours in the rug.

He shook his head. All that was in the past. Finished with. He hunted for the yellow curtains, found them, hung them at the windows. They were far too long for this low-ceilinged room, of course. Tomorrow he'd have to pin them up. For the present, he left them in folds on the ground, unpacked and arranged his books in the dresser, went through to the bedroom and made up the bed, put away his belongings. Then, and only then, did he carry out the intention that had been in the forefront of his mind throughout this bustle of activity. He rang Sophie.

A cool Barbie informed him that Sophie had gone home to Oxford for the week-end, was not expected back until Monday morning. His own disappointment was so intense that he failed to register how strangely unfriendly Barbie had become, simply thanked her and rang off.

No Sophie. He'd imagined her here in the room with him on Sunday, toasting her toes in front of his fire.

Lonely or not, he was hungry, noticed for the first time that it was after eight. He went through to the kitchen, cooked sausages, bacon and eggs, made a pot of coffee, and settled down to some intensive reading. He must be nearly a year behind Giles now, when once he'd been ahead of him. At Eversholt's for the next six months, though, he'd at least have his evenings free from six o'clock. With Louise safely parked out at Hampstead with Willie for the time being, he must begin to put in some steady reading, attend lectures and demonstrations like the rest of them at Eversholt's, which was staffed mainly by overseas graduates working for higher qualifications. Eversholt's had one major advantage. It was within easy reach of all the teaching hospitals and post-graduate centres in London.

When he went to bed it was late, but on Sunday morning he was up early, making himself tea and toast, re-lighting the fire, scrubbing the place through. This took him until a late lunch – more sausages, bacon and egg, more coffee. Afterwards he went for a walk by the railway, returned for more reading. On Monday he'd ring Sophie.

He did this, from Eversholt's before lunch, but he was unlucky enough to catch her at a moment when she and Leo were ploughing through the day's paperwork together. She was crisp and preoccupied. 'Not tonight, no. Or tomorrow, I'm afraid. Wednesday's booked too. I *am* sorry. Is Thursday any good?'

He was losing her. He knew it. She was in demand at the Central, and soon she'd have drifted away from him altogether. He had to fix Thursday, give her his new telephone number, and get off the line.

All week-end, he'd been counting on seeing Sophie in his flat by Monday evening. Now he returned to it dispirited and alone, looked at it without favour. A noisy shabby basement in King's Cross, a greengrocer's family living upstairs, radio and television blaring. Twenty-year-old linoleum on the floor, a rug from a multiple store, and his own battered furniture from the suburban semi-detached which had once been his home. No background for a girl like Sophie, the only daughter of Sir Sheringham Field, the brilliant Oxford professor of neurology.

Nuts. He had to laugh. Sophie didn't give a damn about the fact that he came from a semi-detached in Cheam, or that he was illegitimate, had no knowledge at all of his father. So why should he?

Louise, who did not have illegitimacy to worry about, worried about the semi-detached. Among her other troubles, she had inflated notions as to what her background should have been. And should be now, of course. Admittedly, the Hampstead shop and the flat above it were an enormous improvement on anything he could offer. He had been to the shop soon after Louise had begun work there, to check that it wasn't some junk stall run by hippies smoking pot all day. On the contrary. A glossy, moneyed place, it catered for the affluent tourist. Not all its antiques might be genuine, but they were shining and well-cared for, covered in gold leaf and mirrored in rococo glass, and Willie matched his shop. A square, short, well-covered entrepreneur with a mop of white hair and expensive suiting, he oozed charm and confidence. Nick guessed he would be a dab hand at selling refrigerators to Eskimos, should the need ever arise. Owing, however, to his excellent management of his own affairs, he was likely to go on selling more or less genuine antiques to tourists in Hampstead. Quite where Louise fitted into his schemes Nick hadn't been able to make out, except that she was as decorative as his furniture.

He'd cross-examined Peregrine on this point. He hadn't wanted the experiment to end in disaster, and he'd said so. Peregrine had shrugged in the mannered way he had.

'See no reason why it should. Willie knows what he's doing. He can manage Lulu, if anyone can.'

Nick only hoped this would prove true.

'After all, you've not been any sort of success at looking after her yourself, have you? The girl only needs a firm hand. That Willie can provide. Oh, no funny business, I do assure you. But you couldn't do much for Lulu yourself, could you? Out all day, and that dreadful flat. Poor Lulu. Not exactly her scene, you'll admit.'

'No,' Nick said shortly. Not his either, if it came to that. But during this conversation he learnt something else. Louise had been lying again.

It came out quite casually. 'It would be different if she had the family home to fall back on still,' Peregrine had remarked, veiled accusation apparent. 'A pity you decided to sell the house, in my opinion.'

'I couldn't have lived in it.'

'I suppose not. But you could have kept a housekeeper there, couldn't you? Gone down at week-ends and so on? And Louise would have felt she had something behind her.'

Peregrine had gone on to paint a picture of a tile-hung rambling period house, lovingly restored, central heating and parquet floors, lawns, rose garden, tennis court. Nick, as usual, hadn't the heart to blow the gaff, expose Louise's lies. They were no more than grandiloquent childish dreams, after all, and he allowed Peregrine to go on assuming that he had disposed of some half-timbered Tudor country house for a vast sum. He had smiled wryly to himself. True, the Warings' semi-detached had been set in a group of roads known locally as the Tudor estate. Its one bay, providing a window for their sitting room downstairs and for Matthew and Joanna's bedroom upstairs, had indeed been tiled. But that was as far as it went. The remainder of the accommodation upstairs consisted of the little room over the hall, Nick's, and the room at the back overlooking the patch of garden – hardly the size of half a tennis court – always known as Trish's room. This was the house that had been home to Louise until she was twelve, and to Nick until Joanna's death, when he'd been in his first clinical year as a medical student. Matthew had died two years earlier. The proceeds from the sale of the house represented Nick's total capital, and it was from this that he had financed Louise's treatment, at the clinic in Berkshire.

Clearly, however, Peregrine imagined him to be sitting on a small fortune. 'You inherited everything, I understand,' he had commented. 'Louise, I think, rather feels that was a little unjust. Yes, I'm afraid she does, you know. Rightly or wrongly.' He spread ringed hands tolerantly.

Nick bit back an angry retort, said only 'There isn't much money.'

Peregrine had shot him a covert probing glance. 'Gone, has it?' he asked. 'Money does have a trick of melting like snow in spring.' He had continued to examine Nick furtively, as though he was working something out.

Nick could see that Peregrine undoubtedly imagined him to have squandered some vast inheritance. He set his lips. Peregrine could think what he liked.

Peregrine was watching, saw the obstinacy settle on Nick's features, recognized the expression. This was how Louise looked when he could do nothing with her. Fundamentally, they were the same, this brother and sister, he decided. Nick had had the additional benefit of a stable upbringing, a good education, finally a medical training, and also, according to Louise, all the privileges of the eldest son. But, though superficially

120

he might appear disciplined, controlled, basically he was like Louise. He'd thrown away his career in medicine, for instance, by unreliability. And, according to Louise again, he too took to drugs when life – as it so easily did – became too much for him. He would, presumably (Peregrine knew almost nothing about hospitals), have his own sources of supply.

There were possibilities in Nick Waring, Peregrine told himself, not for the first time. He might prove even more useful than his sister.

CHAPTER SEVEN

NICK AND SOPHIE

Sophie knew nothing of it, but Nick fussed like an anxious housewife over the preparations for her visit on Thursday. On Wednesday he cleaned the flat, on Thursday in his lunch hour he tramped miles to the one good butcher for a pound of steak, bought red wine from Austria, too. Walking homewards that evening he collected a lettuce, together with Satsumas and black grapes from Tich Bowmaker just before he closed. Then into the flat. In spite of all his efforts, it immediately struck him as bleak, miserable, squalid. Unfit for Sophie. His confidence evaporated. But, determined at least to welcome her with a cheerful blaze, he lighted the fire. Out to the kitchen next, to put potatoes to bake in the oven and open the wine. He took it into the front room, made up the fire, which was crackling nicely, small flames beginning to leap. Now he could begin to watch for Sophie. Sud-

122

denly his heart began to sing.

Sophie's heart sang, too. She sailed along the dreary road in the murky winter evening, in the suede jacket with the soft pale collar and cuffs – hardly adequate, in fact, to keep her warm in the damp chill, but Nick liked it, so she wore it. Even the squalid road made no impact on her today. She was faintly aware that she had reached a rowdy slum, that Giles would say. 'I told you so,' that Barbie would be horrified if she could see the place, that even Leo might be dubious, to say the least. But none of this mattered.

She began to scan the numbers. Twenty-three, and then down the steps to the basement, Nick had said on the telephone.

She went down them, and she could see the firelit room waiting for her. Nick opened the door before she had reached the ground. She flew into his arms. He held her tightly, while they kissed as no one had ever kissed before, as though it were the last kiss on earth, she thought, or the first.

Finally they separated, only to reach out again for one another. At last, hands clasped still, they walked together from the tiny hall almost under the road into the living room. 'Oh, isn't it lovely?' Sophie exclaimed. 'The gorgeous fire, and all your furniture.'

'You're the lovely part,' Nick told her, smoothing her long hair. 'The place is pretty ropey, I'm afraid.' He drew the curtains across. 'I had to pin these up with safety pins,' he explained. 'There's over a yard to spare.'

'I must hem them for you,' Sophie stated, shining as though she'd been told she'd won a football pool. She looked round. 'Where's your rug?'

'Oh, that. Oh, never mind that for now. Take your coat off, and I'll pour you a glass of wine.' He received the coat from her, touched the fur collar with the tips of his fingers. 'Suits you, this coat. Though you look pretty good without it, I must say.' She was leggy and trim in a camel cashmere sweater and skirt, ropes of wooden beads – his last birthday present – high suede boots.

'You look all right yourself, Nick.'

'Me? You must be joking.'

'Of course I'm not joking.' She reached up and traced the line of his brows, held his face between her two hands and kissed him again. 'I like the look of you,' she said, sighed with deep content, and laid her head on his chest. 'And even more the feel of you.'

His arms were round her again. 'Me too,' he said softly. 'Darling Sophie, I love you so very much.' He held her. All his life, he saw, had been a preparation for this moment. Here in a drab basement off King's Cross the meaning of his days became clear to him for ever. His lips in Sophie's hair, he began murmuring jumbled endearments that went nowhere towards expressing the power of his love.

They sat together on the old sofa in front of the fire, his arm round her still, her hand in his. 'I could stay like this all evening,' he said. 'But I promised you a glass of wine, remember? And some food.'

Sophie stirred. 'Let's just stay like this.'

Eventually Nick roused himself, poured wine into Joanna's best glasses, Waterford and heavy, that she had treasured. He gave Sophie one, took his own and toasted her over it. 'To us,' he said.

'To us,' Sophie agreed. Her face was radiant in the firelight's glow, her eyes huge, and the cut glass sparkled. 'For ever,' she added on a breath.

'For ever,' Nick repeated, very seriously. 'I've no right to ask it of you. But it's for ever, and we both know it.'

They didn't, at this moment, even need to touch. They were so close that the very air joined them.

'And now,' Nick said briskly. 'I shall go and cook the steak. Because it would be a pity to starve to death at this juncture.'

'Such a waste, wouldn't it be? I'll come with you.' Sophie's boots clattered on the linoleum as she came behind him fast, and in this house full of noise it was like no other sound. Upstairs, for once the baby wasn't yelling, but the television was on full blast and the Bowmakers were shouting at each other above it. Outside, the traffic roared and the trains crashed. But here in the basement the sound of Sophie's footsteps following him into the kitchen was the music of paradise, the essence of joy.

Both of them put their glasses down on the draining board, hugged briefly. Nick began to deal with the steak.

Sophie wrinkled her nose. 'There's a delicious smell in here,' she said, sniffing.

'You,' Nick suggested, kissed her again.

'It's potatoes in their jackets.'

'There's a lettuce somewhere, if you felt like doing something with it.' Nick turned the steak.

Sophie cast round, discovered the lettuce, ran the tap. More music in Nick's ears. 'I must be right round the twist,' he commented.

'Um?' Sophie was shaking lettuce enthusiastically.

'Every sound, every movement, seems like some sort of poetry. As if no one had ever made it before, only us, and it's part of us, of both of us at once.'

Sophie accepted this garbled announcement with absolute understanding. 'I've never felt this when I've washed a lettuce before,' she added, pushing her nose, since her hands were occupied – as well as wet – into Nick's shoulder as an expression of her emotion. He responded at once by putting his arm round her, while the steak spluttered joyously.

They took the steak, baked potatoes and a tossed green salad through into the front room, ate in the firelight. Nick poured more wine, they toasted one another again.

'To us.'

'For ever.'

They smiled gravely, held hands between mouthfuls. Afterwards Nick made coffee, they ate Satsumas and grapes, talked on. 'What *has* happened to your rug?' Sophie asked idly. 'I don't see it about anywhere.'

'That bloody Louise sold it,' he said explosively. 'To buy herself a maxi coat and some boots and various other odds and ends.

And that's not all she sold either. The radio went soon afterwards, and my watch, too, one day when I was idiot enough to leave it in the bathroom.'

Sophie stared. 'I didn't know she stole things.'

He grimaced. 'I kept quiet about it. Ridiculous, but I was ashamed, although it's trivial compared with her addiction. But it was the stealing I couldn't bear to talk about. She's done it all her life, poor kid. I only hope she doesn't start pilfering at Hampstead.' He frowned. 'I went there to dinner last night.'

'And how was she?'

'Very bright and poised. Showing off a lot, but then Louise does show off. In a way she's at her best then. It keeps her up to scratch.'

'Presumably it was for Willie's benefit. How do they get on?'

'I didn't think he was terribly nice to her. At least, I wouldn't care to be treated like that myself. Not that Louise seemed to mind.'

'In what way wasn't he nice to her?'

'Almost contemptuous, I thought. Ordered her about, you know, rather as if she were a delinquent child.'

'About what she is.'

'Yes. But all the same … however, I'm bound to say she didn't appear to resent it. He certainly kept her on the hop, which was quite good for her. "Louise, go and help Mrs Heneage." "Louise, bring sherry." "Louise, take the chocolates round." "Louise, take your brother down and show him the shop."'

'Do you suppose she'll start stealing from the shop?'

He nodded. 'Afraid so. It's one of the events I expect to hear about daily. It's only a question, as I see it, of which happens first. Whether Willie sacks her, as soon as she stops bothering to be on her best behaviour, or whether she starts picking up Willie's *objets d'art* and flogs them. Though in fact probably both events will coincide. As soon as she can't be bothered to make an effort, Willie will begin disapproving of her, and Louise will know she's slipping. That's when she'll start helping herself to his property. I wish I didn't think it was all going to happen, but I do. And not only will she be back on my hands, miserable and upset, too, but I'll have to reimburse Willie for whatever she's taken. Probably be damned expensive.'

'Poor Nick. What a sister to be saddled with.' She touched his cheek lovingly.

He kissed her. 'Sophie darling, I've no

right to drag you into this mess. No right at all. You don't realize…'

'I'd drag you into my troubles.'

Nick chuckled. 'Only you haven't any. I'm the one with troubles. And how. I didn't mean to come near you until I'd sorted them out, you know.'

'Why on earth not?'

'Well, I thought – I mean – after all…'

'I know exactly what you mean. But you'd better start treating me like an adult human being, Nick Waring. Someone you share problems with. Not just some twitty bird to be taken out.'

'Of course I don't think of you like that.' This of course was true, though why he thought the truth might be usefully under-lined by putting his arm round Sophie again, his lips in her long blonde hair, he would hardly have been able to explain.

'Then don't treat me like that.' Sophie's answer started out brisk, but with each word it grew warmer and slower, until she sounded lovingly indulgent. By now she was curled up against Nick in a manner fast becoming familiar to them both.

Much later, she reminded him lazily. 'Louise is our problem. Both of us have to look after her. She'll be with us for life, and we're not going to allow her to get us down. Because we're together, and that's all that matters.'

'All that matters,' Nick mumbled into her neck. He held her more tightly and added, 'Blow Louise, anyway.'

'Blow Louise,' Sophie repeated, and kissed him. 'You know,' she added, 'It's quite mad, but I feel as if nothing could go wrong ever again. As if we're both suddenly immune to anything life can do, nothing can touch us ever again, because we have each other.' She didn't understand, then, how by loving Nick she had given a hostage to fortune.

'I feel the same,' he agreed. 'We're both nut cases, you realize that?'

'Then we'll be nut cases together.'

'In the meantime, we both have to work tomorrow. I'll see you home.'

'Nick,' Sophie said abruptly. 'When shall we see each other again?' She was not going to sit on the end of a telephone, she had decided, waiting for him to ring, ever again. Or so she imagined.

He laughed, his face young and happy. 'Say breakfast tomorrow?' he suggested, then became practical. 'All day Saturday, could you manage?'

'Perfect. I'll come here.'

'I could come and fetch you.'

'Not necessary. What time shall I come? About eleven?'

'I'll have coffee ready for you. You could wear this super little jacket.' He put her into it, and they went out into the darkness of Minster Row and King's Cross in mid-winter. For all they noticed, it might have been Paris in springtime.

Throughout Friday, Nick grinned to himself in every spare moment, and frequently in working moments, too. Sister Bowmaker knew what the cause was, and imparted it widely. 'He had his blonde bird round yesterday evening, see, and I reckon 'e popped the question and madam said yes. Tich and me reckons we'll 'ave a couple again in that flat before you can say knife.'

This was what Sophie thought. On Saturday she popped the question herself. 'Why don't we get married?' she asked over her mug of coffee.

Nick jumped as though he'd been stung. 'Why don't we *what* did you say?'

'You heard. Why don't we get married? What's stopping us?'

'I'm not in a position to marry, as you know very well.' He was curt.

'What sort of position do you imagine

would be in keeping with taking on the estate of matrimony, may I inquire?' She was imitating the pedantry of the professor of medicine at the Central, but her eyes brimmed with laughter.

Nick didn't agree it was a joke. 'A proper job and the problem of Louise sorted out,' he said briefly.

'Which it never will be. You said that yourself. We have to tackle Louise together. And what do you want another job for? You've got a six months contract. Are you waiting until you've been appointed to a consultant post in ten years' time?'

'You couldn't live here, could you?'

He should have known better than to ask.

'Why on earth not?'

'Why *not?* Good grief, Sophie, look around you.'

'If you can live here, so can I.'

'Oh, Sophie darling.' He had to take her into his arms again. 'All the same,' he said finally, 'you can't.'

They argued about it on and off, during a quietly domestic day. The quiet, needless to say, was in their minds, not around them. The Bowmakers were hard at it above and British Rail was apparently embarked on a major redistribution of its rolling stock over the week-end. Nick and Sophie went out and shopped for food, came back and rearranged the furniture. Sophie cooked a leg of lamb with roast potatoes and parsnips, made an apple pie with frozen pastry. They sat in front of the fire digesting their meal while Sophie sewed the curtains. 'I don't see why we can't simply get married and live here like this,' she protested. 'I can go on working for Leo, and you would be at Eversholt's. What's wrong with that?'

'It wouldn't do. Your parents would have a fit, for one thing.'

'My parents? What have they got to do with it?'

The argument went round and round. But Sophie got nowhere. Nick remained firm. 'If Louise shows any sign of settling down in Hampstead, and I had a two-year contract – then we might be able to think about it,' he said. 'But I've only another four months, and my guess is that Louise will be back on my hands inside a month.'

He took Sophie to St Anne's Square, kissed her hard and furiously on the door-step, ran down the steps and walked out of the square without looking back.

CHAPTER EIGHT

WILLIE IN HAMPSTEAD

'Louise is missing you,' Peregrine told Nick. He'd telephoned him at Eversholt's. 'Willie says, why not come out and have lunch on Sunday, cheer her up?'

Nick's heart sank. He had intended to spend the day with Sophie.

'You know what Lulu is.' Nick could hear the shrug in Peregrine's voice. 'No good leaving it to her, she'll never get round to ringing you. Or at least not until lunch is on the table, so to speak. And Willie does prefer to know who's going to be there for each meal. So I said I'd have a word with you myself.'

Unwillingly, Nick accepted the invitation. What was going on? Louise seemed to have succeeded in worrying Willie already.

'Good,' Peregrine said. 'I have to be in touch with him about some photography, so I'll tell him you'll be along. Twelve-thirty, he said.'

Nick knew that Peregrine often photographed furniture and *objets d'art* for Willie for catalogues and advertisements in the trade papers. It was a lucrative but less publicised aspect of his work. No smashing models, but good clear photographs, carefully lighted and detailed.

When Peregrine rang Willie, though, on this occasion it was Nick they discussed, not photography. 'I've fixed it, he's coming,' he said. 'I think he imagines Louise is in a state.'

'Well, dear boy, and so she is,' Willie said. 'I'm trying to discipline her a little, and she's not too pleased, I can tell you. However, it should have blown over by Sunday.'

'Do you want me to be there?'

'Oh, I don't think so. No need. I want to give him the once-over in more depth than I was able to when he came before. We had other people here, then, if you remember. And at that time I had no idea you had plans for him, either. Frankly, you know, I'm not entirely easy in my mind about it. He might easily prove a liability.'

'He may be a liability to his hospital,' Peregrine retorted, 'and from what I've been able to gather, he is. But hardly to us. I'd have thought he'd be a distinct acquisition.'

'Allow me to form my own judgment about the matter, dear boy. After all, we can't afford to make mistakes.'

'He's been sacked from his job at the Central London Hospital, he's working down at Eversholt's Hospital in a temporary post only – a month at a time is all he can get – and he's living in a basement in King's Cross. Minster Row. I've been past in the car to have a look, and its dire. If you ask me, he's being handed to us on a plate. We ought to grab him.'

'He is still working, though. He's keeping up some sort of a front.'

'I never said he was down and out. He'd be no use to us if he couldn't function, would he? I simply said he was on the downward path. He's penniless and a bit desperate. All we have to do is step in at the psychological moment, and...'

'I know what your impressions are. But can we afford to rely on them, go ahead and commit ourselves?'

'I did my homework, Willie. I told you.' Peregrine was urgent. Willie was a fool if he let Nick Waring slip through his fingers. After all, it wasn't every day one stumbled across a fully-trained doctor ripe for picking. 'I talked to that friend of his, Giles Stanstead, you know. I'd met him in Nick's flat when I took Lulu back one evening, when they were still in St Anne's Square, and I made a point of running into him in the King's Head. That's the pub opposite the Central London Hospital, where all the staff go. I talked to Giles about Nick, told him I knew him because of Louise, you see, and said I was worried about him. He said he was very worried about him, too, and told me exactly what had happened, why Nick lost his job.' He chuckled. 'Pot, is what he thinks it is. These young doctors can be very innocent at times. I didn't disillusion him. Even when they believe it's only pot, though, there's been a fantastic amount of talk about Nick round the hospital. I was staggered. And you should hear what he said about Eversholt's Hospital. None of them would touch a job at the place, apparently.' Peregrine was emphatic. He found Willie's caution a little worrying. To lose Nick, simply through Willie's old-maidish anxieties, would be madness. 'You have to take some risks, or you never get anywhere,' he added. 'Besides, you know what Lulu has always said.' Unfortunately Willie held the purse strings. If he said no, that would have to be the end of it.

'Certainly I know what Louise has told us both. But do we necessarily believe her? Pull yourself together, dear boy.'

'Oh, of course you can never tell, with Lulu, I agree absolutely. But I believe what she says about Nick. Partly because it's confirmed, as I said, by this Giles character. And also because if Lulu was going to lie about Nick, I'd expect her to make him out the success story of all-time. God's gift to surgery. If even Lulu admits he's a hopeless failure, we can assume he is, I'm sure of that. Especially when her opinion coincides with what his friends at the hospital say about him. And what they say is, Nick Waring is finished.'

'Yes, I think there can be very little doubt of that. As you say, the facts bear it out.'

'Well then…'

'That's not what's disturbing me.'

'Lulu says…'

'I've told you what I think about that, dear boy. However, there's no more to be done until I've had a good long talk with him myself.'

When Nick arrived in Hampstead he was greeted with warm friendliness by Willie, wearing his Sunday attire of maroon quilted smoking jacket, braided and frogged. 'Come in, come in, dear boy. Come and get warm by the fire on this intolerably cold day. You young people never seem to me to put on enough clothes for this freezing weather.'

Nick had never believed anyone outside Edwardian novels actually said 'dear boy' like this. But then Willie, clearly, was some sort of Edwardian relic himself. Yet in fact, Nick did a rapid calculation, he could have been no more than a schoolboy when Edward VII died. Presumably he must have had an Edwardian mother, perhaps a grande dame of the period. Her influence would explain Willie. The antiques, his way of life, the mannerisms, even today's maroon smoking jacket. Nick was reasonably satisfied with his neat little case history, unaware that Willie was busily conducting a similar assessment. He pressed madeira on Nick and fussed about with little biscuits, petit fours, even fingers of a rich fruit cake. All set out on lace doilies on little silver dishes, and placed on a series of small mahogany tables, with tooled leather surfaces and piecrust edging. Nick felt all hands and feet, not to mention far too casually dressed in roll-neck sweater, anorak and jeans.

He ought to have bought himself another presentable suit for occasions like this, he realized, as he sipped the madeira, ate the excellent fruit cake. His only suit, which he'd bought with considerable care shortly before he qualified, had been sold by Louise in one of her moments of penury. She'd obtained virtually nothing for it, either, to his fury, and had been noticeably unrepentant. No one, she assured him, wore grotty old objects like that any longer. Apparently she'd done him a good turn. He could find himself some more trendy gear, look like a human being for a change.

At the time he hadn't replaced the suit, seeing only too clearly that unless he kept it locked up the incident would be repeated, he would merely have thrown more money away. Except for the first interview at Eversholt's – when he'd borrowed one from Giles – he hadn't needed a suit recently. But he couldn't go on indefinitely like this, especially if he was intending to go on teaching rounds and lectures. And obviously it would have been far more appropriate if he'd had a suit for this Sunday lunch with Willie. He saw the acute little eyes raking him, wondered what Willie was thinking. He seemed extraordinarily friendly, began to draw Nick out.

Nick was perfectly able to recognize what was happening, of course. For some purposes of his own, Willie was extracting his *curriculum vitae* as certainly as if he had demanded it set out on foolscap, thirty roneoed copies for an appointments board. But he did it with such friendliness and warmth, such a depth of understanding sympathy, almost paternal affection, that Nick could not prevent himself from responding like a shy boy to a kindly uncle. Or, in fact, a father-figure. Louise's attitude became comprehensible now. Was Willie, then, preparing to be his father, too?

It seemed like it.

There were embarrassing moments, of course. Willie, for instance, turned out to be under the same misapprehension as Peregrine about the Waring family mansion. Nick cursed Louise silently for her childish fairy tales, again could not bring himself to let her down. Unfortunately, though, this left Willie assuming that somehow or other Nick had managed to dissipate a fortune. He made one attempt to extricate himself from the misunderstanding. 'It was actually quite a small house,' he explained. 'And it was sold before the market went haywire.'

Willie had agreed gently, almost forgivingly, and Nick saw that his comment had been received as merely the sign of a guilty conscience.

'It's a pity, though, you couldn't have kept it on for Louise's sake,' he remarked next. 'She needs a home, poor child.'

Louise came first. Willie's opinion of her mattered. Nick was quite prepared to let him believe her hard-done-by, neglected by everyone, if this would encourage Willie himself to go on caring for her. Nick had only to look round this well-kept flat, compare it with the slum he lived in, to know that Louise was better off with Willie.

She appeared at this point, and Nick scanned her clinically, didn't altogether like what he saw. Something was wrong, though she was wearing the tapestry trousers and tabard, with a full-sleeved shirt in deep clover chiffon that set off her dark beauty. Astonishingly, she had attained elegance. Another of Willie's achievements. But she remained edgy and tense, and darted quick stabbing glances, covert and intense, at Willie.

At lunch they were joined by the housekeeper, Mrs Heneage, a big handsome woman who towered over Willie. The meal they ate was a dream. A dream that began with subtly-flavoured Vichyssoise, cold and creamy in Worcester porcelain bowls, fragile and delicately coloured, continued with perfectly roasted pheasant, accompanied by crisp and savoury garnishes, potato straws, tiny sprouts in butter. The meal ended unexpectedly with a schoolboy's treat, a mouthwatering treacle tart, that Louise refused but Nick demolished. He hadn't eaten one like it since Joanna died. The ever-observant Willie crowed delightedly. 'Ah, dear boy, we are at one, I perceive. I'm afraid I have a juvenile passion for treacle tart, which Mrs Heneage is kind enough to encourage. I'm glad to see you share my taste.' Greedily he poured cream over a second helping. Pink and perspiring from the superb food and wine coupled with efficient central heating aided by his log fire, he was a jolly Dickensian figure. No one could fail to surrender to his benevolence.

He knew this, of course, and traded on it. But Nick thought he was entitled to this minor blemish in his geniality. Now he was pressing brandy on Nick, while Mrs Heneage poured small cups of strong black coffee.

Reluctantly, since he was sure any brandy offered by Willie would be unforgettable, Nick refused it. They had drunk hock with the pheasant, Sauternes with the treacle tart. He didn't propose to devote the rest of the day to sleeping off Willie's lunch.

'No?' Willie was disappointed. 'Are you sure you won't? Do have some, dear boy. I feel certain you'd enjoy it. No? You are sure? Then you must forgive me if I indulge myself.' He poured, offered none to Mrs Heneage or Louise. In Willie's household the females, though treated to a full dose of his concern, had no priority. Willie regarded them as staff, and never forgot it. He suggested now that he and Nick took their coffee to the fireside, while Mrs Heneage and Louise cleared the table.

Mrs Heneage rose instantly, but Louise, who had become increasingly silent during the meal, sat on, hunched over her plate. Nick had seen her like this often, but he doubted if Willie had, wondered how long he would stand for it. Not at all, was immediately clear. 'Louise,' he enunciated sharply. She jumped to her feet at once. 'Yes,' she said quickly. 'Yes, I'm just going. I'll clear.' She half ran into the kitchen, her expression suddenly avid, eager.

Momentarily Nick knew extreme brotherly irritation, no more. But then, with a flash of despair, certainty hit him. Louise was back on the hard stuff. She had been overdue for a fix. He knew the signs too well. Now she had escaped to get herself what her body was

145

crying out for.

It jolted him to the core. She was back on heroin. A death sentence. She had been freed from her dependence on the drug once, but here she was, in spite of all his efforts, back on it. The outlook became more hopeless, more inevitable. He had told Sophie this was what he expected, yet now that it had happened, he knew he had been hoping still for a permanent cure.

What was he to do?

Did Willie know? Had he found out? Was this why Nick had been summoned? Did he at least suspect?

Impossible to believe he did. He sat in his chair, benign and rosy, polished shoes poised on an embroidered footstool by the Adam fireplace, taking little sips of brandy and chatting about wine and food. The gourmet at home.

For a second Nick considered blurting out his fears, of concealing nothing, asking Willie's help. But he rejected the notion at once. So Willie was kind, all right. But he was also sheltered, protected, and above all, elderly. In fact, an old fuss-pot. He was devoted to himself. He liked good wine, good food, good furniture, everything about him just so. He had an excellent housekeeper to see to his comfort, and a beautiful girl, Louise, to help his housekeeper in the flat and at the same time save Willie a few chores in the shop. If he discovered Louise was a drug addict, Nick suspected she'd be out of his household with the speed of light. Men like Willie never wanted any unpleasantness.

Nick's own best plan at present would be to lie low, say nothing. Here in this cosy Hampstead flat Louise was well looked after. The right course now was to await events, to take no action himself. He had often advocated this in hospital, to patients and relatives. He had had no idea how hard it would be to follow. He wanted to do something now. Anything.

At this point Louise came back into the room.

She'd had a fix, he was sure of it.

She began teasing Willie gently, like a devoted, affectionate daughter, and Willie responded, smiled back at her, obviously enjoyed her attention, his earlier sharpness apparently forgotten. Perhaps he'd simply thought her a little moody, was relieved to see her back to her usual spirits. She had come to collect their coffee cups, she told them, and after some lighthearted cajolery, almost Victorian badinage, she took the cups away to the kitchen. Nick watched her go. What the hell was he going to do about her?

Willie watched her go, too. 'A dear child,' he told Nick, his archaic manner even more evident. 'I'm afraid she is a little over-tired today. She does too much. She likes to do this modelling for Peregrine, as you know, and I agreed to release her for it when he needed her. But it tires her out.'

That's when she got the heroin, of course. From Peregrine, Nick saw it all. He should have seen it long ago. What a fool he'd been not to spot it.

'She had two days with him last week.' Willie's voice bore him out. 'And the poor child's tired out as a result. But she does enjoy it so much.' His eyes met Nick's, with benevolent tolerance. 'I haven't the heart to stand in her way.'

Nick knew exactly how Willie felt. This was just how he himself reacted to Louise.

'She's off with him again for three days next week,' Willie was continuing. 'The two of them are going to do some work for a magazine supplement, down in Kent or Sussex. Bodiam, would it be? With some bits of gauze and chiffon nonsense for an advertising feature, they tell me.'

'Louise likes that sort of thing,' Nick agreed. At that moment he almost confided in Willie. Asked him, above all, not to let her go off with Peregrine. But in fact he stuck to his earlier decision, said nothing. But later, walking downhill to the tube station in the early dusk of the winter afternoon, he wished he had followed his first impulse and told Willie the whole story.

He'd been a fool. Louise needed help. Watchful care. Should he go back now, uphill again to Willie and his fireside, unload the facts frankly on to him, take his advice?

But how could be begin? What reason could he give for reappearing? Louise would want to know why he'd returned – how would he get rid of her?

He could telephone first, of course, explain to Willie that he needed to talk to him privately, without Louise. That would be the way.

Arrived at the tube station, he shut himself into a telephone box.

CHAPTER NINE

JUNKIE

'Yes,' Paul Worsley said. 'I did warn you, you remember.' He shifted papers about on his desk, frowned.

'Oh, you warned me all right,' Nick agreed. 'And I warned myself, too. But it's still a blow when it actually hits you.'

'Of course.' Paul shook his head. 'It's a blow to me every time it happens to a patient. And none of them happens to be my sister. At least Anne's not that daft.'

'Most of them don't come quite as daft as Louise. And just as well, isn't it?'

'Most of them don't have her upbringing. Luckily for them.'

They were talking in the drug treatment centre. Nick had rung Paul from Hampstead on the off-chance that – since at the drug treatment centre they worked all hours – he might be on duty. Paul had been there. 'Pop round, Nick,' he'd said at once. 'I'm on all night, and it's quiet so far, so come along

150

and get it off your chest.'

'You mustn't blame yourself,' he said now, out of the blue.

Nick regarded him bleakly. 'I haven't exactly been much help to her, have I?'

'No one can help someone like Louise. You know that as well as I do. She was hopelessly messed about in childhood by an immature and selfish mother. Now she's selfish and immature herself, and in addition deeply disturbed. That's my opinion – you may not realize quite how disturbed she is. But I think the poor girl is pretty far gone.' He sighed. 'There's no future for people like that. We both know Louise will be lucky if she's alive five years from now. If an overdose doesn't carry her off, infection is almost bound to, or she'll succumb to some minor illness that she won't have the strength to fight. The outlook is pretty hopeless for all these addicts.' Then, unexpectedly, he smiled. An ironic, self-mocking, yet surprisingly gentle smile. 'But here I am,' he said. 'Giving up my days and far too many of my nights as well, trying to prop them up. Somewhere inside me I remain convinced there is a future, there's hope for at least a few of them, if only a few of us can give everything we have to give. Often it's nothing but a bloody waste of time.

When I'm feeling optimistic, though, I think it's a crusade. But...' he thumped his desk forcefully, 'but we're mugs, you and I, Nick, to imagine we can make any real difference. Let's face it, usually the most we can do is postpone the inevitable for a year or two. So stop blaming yourself.'

'My head knows you're right,' Nick admitted.

'It's not our heads that are the trouble. We're both quite competent up here.' He tapped his own forehead. 'It's our sloppy old hearts that need seeing to. Face it, Nick, there's very little you or anyone can do for Louise. She's been on heroin before, we got her off, kept her off for a short while. Now she's on again.'

'Or I assume she is,' Nick pointed out. 'And her behaviour fits. But I couldn't go as far as to examine her under this bloke Willie's nose. Or I didn't think I could. I may have been wrong there.'

'If you think she's back on the hard stuff I've no doubt she is. At any rate we should make plans on that basis. Now, you know the pharmacology as well as I do. Once she's on heroin, even for quite a short period, she's physically dependent. Her body needs it. But while her supplies hold out, she won't be in too bad a state. So there's not much chance of weaning her off it while she has access to a reliable source of supply.'

'Which, as I said, I feel certain is that blasted photographer, Peregrine Caversham.'

'Yes.'

'That's why I was wondering if I ought to confide in Willie. He's her new father-figure.'

'And a father-figure is what she needs most of all. A kindly, accepting father-figure.'

'Which I have failed to provide.'

'My dear idiot, of course you have. You're her brother, you're – how much older than she is?'

'Eight years.'

'Nothing. She can quarrel and fight with you as if you were both in the nursery still.'

'And does,' Nick agreed with a twisted smile.

'And does. There you are, then. You're a crutch she can use in emergencies, the only member of her family who's reliable. You're always there when she needs you. But you'll never be the father she's looking for. Doubtful, of course, if anyone ever will. That's her tragedy. Or part of it.' He shook his head. 'I'm afraid it's really far too late to help her much now.'

'However, I intend to go on trying,' Nick

said. 'So what do I do next?'

'I wish I knew, mate. Useless to approach this photographer. He's probably as big a liar as the rest of them. Anyway, he's not going to lay off her because you ask him to. Nothing to be obtained from him. Short of transporting her forcibly out of London to undergo treatment, you won't be able to separate her from her source of supply. It was different before. When she left Spain, she was cut off automatically from her supply. She had no funds, so she was obliged to accept your solution, go for treatment. And once she'd had the treatment, she does seem to have made some sort of attempt to steer clear of the stuff to begin with. But it didn't last.'

'Nothing Louise does ever lasts. At present there's no doubt she's quite well placed with Willie in Hampstead. He seems to be able to control her, and it's a very comfortable well organized flat. It might easily be a lot worse.'

'So long as the system continues to work, I don't think she should be disturbed.' Paul sighed again. 'Just keep in touch, sit it out. It's all you can do.'

'Tell me,' Nick said abruptly. 'What do you think are the chances it might help her if I put Willie in the picture?'

154

'I shouldn't do it, Nick. That's my advice. Most people won't have anything to do with the drug scene if they can avoid it. And can you blame them? No, I wouldn't say anything to him.'

Nick grinned sarcastically. 'At present, I rather imagine Willie is under the impression that I'm the monster who led Louise into all her difficulties.'

Paul nodded. 'She's been feeding him a load of rubbish about you, no doubt. All addicts lie like troopers, whether it's necessary or not. Tell me more about this photographer, though.'

'Peregrine? She met him ages ago. He smokes pot, that's all I've ever noticed, I'm afraid. I don't care for him, for what that's worth. Never have.'

'Do you think he's an addict? Or simply a pusher? Or both, as they mostly are?'

'Certainly he's not a junkie of the drop-out sort. A very hard worker, to be fair to him. Never lets up. Drives himself. If he's a pusher, I'm bound to say I feel very angry indeed. Not only with him, though. With myself most of all. For letting it happen under my nose. Damn it, I was supposed to be looking after the girl.' Nick's face hardened into lines of cold determination. 'If he's got Louise back on heroin, while he steers clear of it himself, it's unforgivable.'

'You've no proof that he's responsible. It could be almost anyone.'

'Yes. It could be. Well, I'm going to find out.' Nick rose to his feet, stood over the desk, tall, thin, intensely angry. 'That'll give me something to follow up while I have to remain inactive as far as Louise is concerned.'

'Hey, watch your step, boyo,' Paul said quickly.

'Eh?'

'You keep out of it. You'll be in big trouble if you start following up the pushers, laddie. It's a very lucrative rotten old trade. Hellish dangerous. Lethal, it can be. Don't meddle. Not at any price.'

'No need to panic. I'm only thinking of investigating Peregrine, nothing else.'

'Don't do it, Nick.' Paul was urgent.

'I'm simply going to keep my eyes open and my ears pinned back,' Nick said. 'Nothing in it.'

'Watch it.'

'Will do. And thanks for all your advice. And your time. See you.'

'Be careful,' Paul repeated. Worried, he watched Nick leave. He seemed to regard investigating Peregrine as a sideline. But it could be dangerous, Paul knew. Louise, he was afraid, was already a lost cause, but trying to look after her had cost Nick his post at the Central, and Paul didn't at all care for the possibility that was in his mind. Before he was through Louise might cost Nick his life.

As Nick came out of the clinic entrance, began to pick his way between the junkies hanging around the building, a yellow Triumph Spitfire passed. In it, Giles and Sophie, who had been down to the coast for the day.

Nick, preoccupied, didn't recognize the car or its occupants, but Giles saw him, glanced quickly at Sophie. Evidently she had noticed nothing, and he drove on to St Anne's Square, left her there without mentioning Nick. Worried and disturbed at the latest complication, he dropped in at the King's Head to restore himself before going into the Central.

He'd had a hard knock that day. Sophie had broken the news to him of her approaching marriage to Nick. It was all settled, only the date remained to be fixed, she'd said. She'd told Giles a certain amount about Louise, too, and at the time he'd believed her. But now he couldn't help wondering what Nick was doing, coming out of the drug treatment centre at that hour on a Sunday evening? Had he dropped in to talk to them about Louise? Surely he could have done that on the telephone? It was possible of course that Louse had been admitted after an overdose. That would account for Nick's presence. But Giles couldn't help asking himself if anything Nick had told Sophie was true? Who was the patient, Nick or Louise? Or both of them? Wherever the truth might lie, Giles hated to think of Sophie involved in so much unhappiness. He'd been right all along, Nick was no good to her.

In the King's Head he found friends, unburdened himself, spoke at length of his anxiety for Sophie, about to ruin her life. When Peregrine, in search of background information to reinforce his case with Willie, dropped in there, the talk was still about Sophie and Nick. Peregrine lapped it up, went straight home and rang Willie.

'Very enlightening, dear boy,' Willie said. 'Most useful. My meeting with Nick, too, went well. I think now we know where we stand.'

'I always felt sure…'

'I know, Perry, I know. And I must admit you were absolutely right. But I do like to feel my way.'

'So now what?'

'So now I think we should have a little talk about our future plans. I agree with you, Nick can be extremely useful to us.'

'I'm glad you think so,' was all Peregrine said. But there was an unmistakable ring of triumph in his voice.

'Festina lente,' Willie warned him at once. 'Let us hasten slowly. Caution above all, dear boy. Suppose we have a talk tomorrow, before you go down to Folkestone?'

'I'll come over,' Peregrine promised.

The next morning he found Willie ensconced in front of a roaring fire, a table with hot coffee and milk in Queen Anne silver awaiting Peregrine's arrival. 'Ah, dear boy, come along and warm yourself. Draw your chair up to the fire. I've told Mrs Heneage we mustn't be disturbed, and Louise will stay down in the shop.'

'She'll do that all right. I locked the door as I came through.'

'Excellent. I'm glad you did that. It's because we don't neglect these simple precautions that our affairs are prospering. As I think we can say they are.'

Peregrine gave a thumbs-up sign with a broad grin, adding: 'So now you agree we can go ahead and take Nick on?'

'I really think we can, dear boy. I've come to the conclusion you are right about him. He should be most useful.'

'I thought you'd see it, when you came to know him.'

'He won't be as easy to handle as Louise, I'm afraid. Not dependent on us in the same way. But we may be able to get over that. I think we'll have to pay him a good deal more in actual cash, too. But we'll be doing very comfortably ourselves, so we mustn't grudge it.'

'He'll be worth a lot more than poor Lulu.'

'Don't forget, Perry, that without Louise we would never have been put in touch with our suppliers. And then where would we be?'

'Nowhere.'

'Quite so. However, thanks to you, we have the distribution very well organized. So what I want to do in future is send Nick over to France once a month. Let him do the laboratory work, bring it over ourselves. No middle man.'

They looked at one another.

'We can do it, easily,' Peregrine said. 'We've shifted enough antiques across the Channel.

Child's play to bring the heroin in ourselves. Furniture out. Heroin in. Bingo.'

'We are going to touch real money at last,' Willie said reverently. 'We must be careful, though, not to lose our heads. That would be fatal. In fact, before we go any further, I'm convinced there is one more precautionary step we should take. This is the way I propose we should go about it.'

Peregrine drank his Blue Mountain coffee and listened. He doubted if what Willie suggested was necessary. But Willie always liked to make sure he had the upper hand. Peregrine shrugged. 'I don't mind doing it,' he said. 'If it makes you happy.'

'It's not a question of making me happy.' Willie was sharp. 'Our aim must be to discredit him completely, so that he knows he has no road back. I want him to lose all confidence in himself, too. Once he's right down, then I shall be there to extend the helping hand in his hour of need.' Willie twinkled, sipped his creamy coffee in the Crown Derby cup. 'From then on, he'll be our man, and once we have him, he'll be invaluable. In more ways than one. But I don't want to approach him until we can be absolutely sure of him.'

'All right,' Peregrine fingered his beads

lovingly, recollected, too, Nick's disparaging glances at his gear. 'I daresay it would be useful. And I must say, I wouldn't mind seeing him taken down a peg myself.'

'Suppose we put our plan into action as soon as you return then?'

'Thursday.'

Nick accepted Willie's invitation to dinner without hesitation. Another meeting would give him an opportunity to study both Peregrine and Louise after their trip. This word, he was afraid, would prove only too appropriate a description of their travels.

There was a rush of work at Eversholt's that week, and it was after five on Thursday evening before they saw daylight. Not until then did Nick remember that he'd intended to buy something respectable to wear for Willie's dinner party. He'd done nothing about it. Sister Bowmaker, though, would know what to do. She had all the answers. 'What on earth shall I do, sister? Here I have this dinner party I must go to in Hampstead, and only jeans to turn up in. I meant to go shopping one lunch hour, but it hasn't been that sort of week. Not a chance.'

'Late shopping today, doctor,' she reminded him. 'Why don't you 'op on the Victoria Line, go to Oxford Circus. You'll be there in no time, and you're bound to be able to find something suitable, even if it's only a smart pair of dark trousers and one of them stripey shirts.'

She was right, as usual. A suit might be essential for ward rounds, but what she suggested would do very well for Willie's flat.

He ended up with a couple of pairs of sombre trousers, a corduroy jacket, and two shirts, one lilac and one pale blue, both with silvery damask stripes, and was at home in Minster Row by seven, with enough time to change. The new look for Nick Waring, he thought, grinning at himself in the mirror, rather pleased, wishing only that he was about to join Sophie. However, to Hampstead he had to go, and fast. He reached the flat a little breathlessly just after eight, was admitted by Peregrine, who gave him an odd look.

They went upstairs together, and Willie gave him the once-over too, the same swift scrutiny, he was amused to see. He smiled to himself. It must be his new gear.

Louise came in, wearing a long violet dress with trumpet sleeves and wide scalloped collar in heavy folds. She greeted his appearance with no inhibitions. 'Nickie darling, how super you look. New shirt? I like.'

'You too,' he said. 'Gorgeous.'

Willie and Peregrine crossed glances for the second time. Why had he had to smarten himself up like this, today of all days? Behind Nick's back Peregrine – shrugged fatalistically.

Willie offered drinks, began to tell them about dinner. Savoury smells were already coming from the kitchen. 'Mrs Heneage has prepared a jugged hare,' he informed them. 'In order that we may do full justice to it, I thought simply a little consommé first. Then after dinner, before Nick and Peregrine have to face this far too seasonal weather, I might make some of my warming punch.' He beamed cherubically round, his only ambition their comfort and enjoyment, while they made the appropriate gratified noises. No doubt about it, Nick thought, there was something immensely likeable about Willie. Easy to see why Louise had picked him out to give her the home and background she longed for.

He tried to concentrate on Peregrine, but Willie's benevolence came between them. At Eversholt's, too, Nick had had a busy, tiring week. In addition he'd been out with Sophie one evening, while the other two he'd spent

164

at postgraduate lectures. Now on Thursday here in Willie's cosy flat, he found it impossible to bring his exhausted mind to bear on the problem of Peregrine. Yet this, he reminded himself, was why he had chosen to come.

The excellent food and the warmth of the flat were no help. Dinner was delicious – jugged hare, with forcemeat balls and redcurrant jelly, accompanied by a claret that Willie had decanted into a cut glass claret jug with silver mountings. They all, except for Louise – who maintained that she had to watch her figure or Peregrine would sack her – had second helpings of the hare. Nick saw that his plate, a green-banded porcelain with posies of summer flowers, was different from the equally delicate china he had eaten off the previous Sunday, and asked Willie about this.

'Dear boy, how acute of you to notice.' Willie beamed. 'I must make a confession, though. It's stock, I'm afraid. Whenever I buy in something that particularly takes my fancy, I can't resist using it at my own table. Mrs Heneage is very patient with me, and takes the greatest care of this lovely stuff. Otherwise I wouldn't dare risk it, of course.'

'What is it, Willie? Spode?' Peregrine was

turning his plate in his hands, squinting up from below at its base.

'Careful, dear boy. No, not Spode. A *leetle* more valuable.' He looked archly round the table. 'Any other suggestions?' He turned down all that were made, refused to divulge what the plates were. 'They could be Meissen,' he teased them happily. 'Or Sèvres, perhaps?'

His guests obediently adopted expressions of impressed puzzlement.

'How shall I bear to let them go,' Willie admitted, 'I can't imagine. I do like to have nice things round me, I must say. However, that's enough trade talk, I'm boring you all, I'm afraid. Tell me about Kent. Was it very cold in the depths of the Weald? I'm afraid it must have been.'

'Freezing,' Louise assured him, shuddering. 'And Peregrine would insist on me standing for hours on end on the drawbridge at Bodiam in horrid chiffon. Truly terrible.'

'Very good pictures we got, though,' Peregrine said confidently. He described how flashes of inspiration had transformed the pictures he'd planned into an outstanding series of fashion photographs that might make his name. Alight with triumph, his

166

eyes glittered and his ringed hands gesticu-
lated. Nick, unfairly, disliked him more than
ever.

'All this resulted in more standing about,
you may be sure,' Louise complained. 'I only
hope the results are going to be as groovy as
you say, Perry darling. Because I'm sure I
shall have rheumatism for the remainder of
my days.'

'Rheumatism?' Nick repeated. 'Where?'

'Oh, don't take me up like that, Nickie,
please. I can't bear it when you go all pro-
fessional on me.'

Peregrine and Willie crossed glances again.
They were sitting round the fire drinking
coffee now, and Willie changed the subject.
'These cups are Crown Derby,' he instructed
them. 'Middle period, you know. I found
them when I went to a sale outside Notting-
ham recently, to look at some pictures. It was
rather interesting. The pictures were quite
dreadful, but...' he went on to tell them
about sales he had attended up and down
the country, until his little gilt clock chimed
the half hour. 'Nine-thirty,' he stated. 'I think
it's time for me to make my punch. Louise
will help me, won't you, my dear? Because I
think you two children...' he indicated
Louise and Peregrine '...both need an early

night, after your arduous travelling. Peregrine, you can give Nick a lift home, can't you, dear boy?'

'Of course. It's on my way, more or less.'

'Thanks very much,' Nick said. 'If you would drop me off at the nearest point, that'll be fine. I can walk the rest.'

Peregrine started to describe, with prolific detail, the exact route he proposed to take across London from Hampstead to Chelsea, Willie and Louise came in with a vast amount of impedimenta for making and serving punch, and a tremendous furore ensued. Finally a potent-smelling brew was ladled by Willie into special glasses in silver holders, and handed round by Louise. 'That's for Peregrine, my dear. Now you've had it before, Perry, but this time I've put a *fraction* more cinnamon in, I think, and an additional measure of rum. 'I've also tried putting a little – well, you must tell me *exactly* what you think. I do *honestly* want to know. Now this one for your brother, Louise. It's fairly spicy, you'll find, Nick. But inspirating, on a cold night, I feel sure you'll agree.'

He agreed, all right. The punch was fierce, aromatic. A curious flavour, but undeniably pleasant, though he wondered if it might not take the skin off his mouth. 'Delicious,' he felt compelled to say, as Willie was eager for praise. The stuff stung his lips, they felt thick and rubbery, and his mouth was beginning to feel as though he'd had a dental anaesthetic. His head started to buzz, while the walls were undoubtedly closing in on him. 'I'm afraid,' he said, putting his glass down carefully on a table, or trying to, only the table began to recede from him into infinity. 'I'm afraid I...'

'Oh dear,' Willie said. 'Oh dear, I'm afraid my punch is a little too powerful for Nick, don't you know? I did wonder if – oh dear, I'm afraid he's not very well. Peregrine, do you think you'd better take him home without more ado?'

'I think that would be the best plan,' Peregrine agreed. 'It is a bit strong, you know, Willie. I knew what was coming, of course, and I had hardly any of your lovely claret. But I fear Nick didn't quite realize – I expect the fresh air will revive him, you know. Look, old man, if you just lean on me we'll go downstairs, shall we?'

Nick came to his feet obediently, making some incoherent comment.

'I'll go first,' Willie suggested. 'And lead the way. Open the door for you, too. Louise, you'd better go straight to bed. Peregrine and I will see your brother's all right, poor fellow.'

'Oh, poor Nickie.'

'Off to bed, Louise.'

'Silly thing, how could he?' The door shut behind her.

'I take it Andy will be ready for you?' Willie asked, as they negotiated the stairs.

'He'll be waiting in the car. I told him to be there by half past nine.'

'I'll leave you to manage then,' Willie said, with relief, opening the street door. 'Get that jacket off him, won't you? Far too prosperous.'

'Not to worry, Andy and I will cope.'

The door shut behind them.

Andy materialized. 'Need any assistance, Perry?'

'Yeah, Come round the other side. He's passing out fast. Better get him into the back of the car. You come in the front with me.'

'You don't think I ought to go in the back, too? To keep an eye on him?'

'Not necessary. He only wants to die. Don't you, Nick?'

A thick rambling mumble came from the stooping, swaying figure.

170

'You'll be able to lie down in a minute, then you'll feel a bit better.'

Nick caught this. 'Lie down. Be – er.'

'That's it, laddie. In you go. Haul him in, Andy. There we are. Right.' Peregrine slammed the back door, went round to the driver's seat, while Andy let himself in on the passenger side. The Citroën moved off.

'We'll go round to one of those quiet roads down in the Vale of Health.' Peregrine turned the car into a curving tree-lined road.

Quiet and still, the sound of London's traffic was muted here. They might have been in a peaceful village lost in the country. 'Now we'll give him the next instalment.' Peregrine pulled the Citroën in to the road-side. 'First of all, though, we must rough him up a bit. Wouldn't you know he'd have to choose tonight to appear as chic as some trendy actor? We'll have to get that shirt off him, as well as the jacket. No junkie'd own a nice clean extravagant shirt like that. See if you can find that old shirt of mine I use for wiping around. See it anywhere about? We can put that on him instead. It's torn, but that won't matter. So much the better, in fact. Get some dirt and engine grease and so on over him, too. Come on, Nick, give me a hand, can't you?' he added impatiently.

'Don't lie there like a log. I want to get this shirt off. You can sit up and be some use.'

'Si – up. Be some ushe.'

'That's more like it. Now the other arm. Now get it into here. That's the style. Right. You can lie down again now.'

'Lie down,' Nick collapsed on to the floor of the Citroën again.

'Wonder what Willie gave him?' Andy asked. 'Certainly works.' He smeared grease over Nick's face and hair, wiped dust and dirt from the recesses of the boot and off the wheel rim over him. 'There, that's for you. You look a right old mess now, mate.'

'It was a very potent punch Willie brewed up,' Peregrine said. 'I only had a sip or two myself, but I could tell at once that it packed quite a kick on its own. What he added to knock Nick out I don't know, but I should say the two are acting together and proving pretty violent. I hope it's going to be all right still to give him the injection on top of it all.'

'You want to be careful, Perry,' Andy warned. 'You said you didn't want to finish him off. I'd go a bit carefully, if I was you.'

'Not to worry. I am going carefully. Let's have your arm, then, Nick. Right. In she goes.' He sighed with relief. 'That's done. Off we go, then.'

CHAPTER TEN

LEO

Leo Rosenstein had been up to the intensive care unit to see a patient he'd operated on that morning. The patient was doing nicely, and Leo was on his way home. He came out of the side entrance to the General Surgical Block, cut through St Anne's Gardens – a route much used by junior and senior surgical staff alike, leading as it did not only to Harley Street, but to the King's Head and Giovanni's, the small Italian restaurant next door. As he bounced busily through the gardens, Leo glanced at his watch. Early enough to miss the returning throng, with any luck. At eleven the King's Head would empty, and Giovanni's too, residents would come pouring through the gardens to the surgical block for their final rounds. But he should be away before this minor rush-hour set in.

He was just congratulating himself when he saw something that failed to please him in any way whatsoever. Slumped on the seat at the entrance to the gardens he saw a slight, dirty, drooping but only too familiar figure. His former house surgeon. Filthy, shabby, unkempt. This reality was much worse than anything Leo had imagined when they'd kept warning him that Waring had dropped out.

As Leo drew nearer, he noticed that Waring was muttering to himself. 'Bloody punsh,' he caught as he came up to him. He squinted up, spotted Leo. 'Shir,' he said with dignified formality, began to rise to his feet, only to crumple. Leo caught the slight swaying form, held Nick firmly, lowered him on to the wooden seat again. Waring, who had always been thin, was nothing but skin and bone now. So they'd all been right about him. Only Leo himself, because he'd been fond of the lad, seen a considerable future for him, had dealt in as much wishful thinking as Sophie.

'Yer stoopid nit,' he said with bitter fury. 'If yer must get stoned, why the 'ell come 'ere?'

'Come here?' Nick repeated vaguely. 'Wheresh here?' He peered about through half-shut eyes. 'Head feelsh tebble. 'Terr-ib-ib-able. No. Tebb...'

'Be quiet.' Leo bit the words off. He had never lacked authority, and the order penetrated through the fog. Nick closed his lips, said no more.

Leo, known for rapid decisions, had made one already. The least he could do. One last service for Waring, and after that he hoped he'd never set eyes on him again. He slung Nick's arm over his own bulky shoulders, took him in a grip of iron. 'Walk, Waring, damn you.' The words came gratingly. Nick walked. More of a stumble, but with Leo holding him upright they managed to cover the ground with formidable speed. Out of St Anne's Garden, sharp left into the Central's forecourt, where Leo had a parking space. No one about, which was more than the young idiot deserved. Leo dived for his keys, performing a complicated balancing act, unlocked the Jaguar, opened the passenger door. 'Git in.' Nick collapsed on to the seat, Leo slammed the door, locked it from the outside, walked round to the driving seat, started the engine, drove out.

'Made it,' he commented to himself. 'Blooming young fool.' He turned into Tottenham Court Road, began working his way towards King's Cross. Sophie had told him about the flat in Minster Row, and he required only to extract the number from Nick, now apparently lapsed into stupor. 'What number's your flat, Waring?'

No reply.

'Answer me, blast you. I asked you a question, Waring.'

Nick tried to pull himself together. He must be on one of Leo's teaching rounds. Leo was in a rage, too. 'Shir?' he inquired politely.

'*What number?*'

'Number?' Number, number. Number of what? How ghastly. He couldn't have been attending. And Leo in one of his moods, too. 'Number, shir? I'm afraid I don't...'

'Number of your flat.'

'Oh. Flat.' Odd question, on a teaching round. Still that's what he'd said. 'Twelve, Shaint Annesh Shquare.'

'Stone the crows.' Leo took a deep breath. 'Minster Row, this is *Minster Row.*'

'Oh, Minshter Row. Yesh. Um.' Of course, he lived in Minster Row now. He knew that. Why had he thought...? What the hell had he thought, anyway? It had gone. But what was Leo doing in Minster Row, of all places? 'What you doing Minshter Row?'

'Trying to get you home, you stoopid clown. Don't ask me why, either, because I

176

don't know. Now let's have a little co-oper-
ation. The number of your flat.'

'Twenny-three.'

'Well, that's a step in the right direction, at
last.' Leo scanned the houses. Nineteen,
then a boarded-up derelict. Twenty-three
must be the newly-painted white one. It
was. Not quite as bad as he'd feared, but
bad enough. 'In the basement, is it?'

'Bashement.'

'Key.'

'Key?'

'Key of your front door.'

Nick shoved his hand into his trouser
pocket, brought it out holding, to Leo's surprise and relief, a key ring. Leo took it from
him, went down the area steps, tried keys
until he found the right one, let himself in,
turned lights on, left doors open behind him,
and collected Nick from the car. He carried
him down the steps ('Ought to 'ave trained
for the bloody ballet'), into the front room,
on to the sofa. He returned to the Jaguar, and
sighing gustily locked it. Across the pavement
again, down the area steps, back into the flat.
He began to prospect, opening doors, switch-
ing on more lights. He discovered the
kitchen, put a kettle on. The place was as neat
and tidy as he would once have expected it to

be. Waring had always been meticulous.

But that didn't fit. Not with the filthy drunk on the sofa, or with the stories he'd been hearing. A discrepancy.

Leo always worried away at discrepancies. Now he wandered round the flat, examining it. Tidy and neat. Clean too. A pair of jeans and a shirt, worn, but much cleaner than the one Nick had on now, thrown on the bed, together with two carrier bags from a department store and a very snazzy lilac shirt. Odder and odder.

The kettle boiled. Leo made strong black coffee, added cold water, took a mug to Nick. 'Drink that. Sit up and drink that.'

Nick sat up, drank, blinked. Handed the mug back. 'Thank you, shir,' he said conscientiously, lay down again, shut his eyes. Leo lifted a lid, frowned, took out his pencil torch, shone it on to the pupil. 'Oh no,' he said flatly. 'Not that too. Oh, Waring, you poor deluded clot.' He put the torch away, walked angrily about the room. 'Just as everyone said,' he muttered. 'Only I thought I knew better. And now what about Sophie? What the muckin' 'ell am I going to say to poor Soph?' He swung on his heel returned to the kitchen, poured another mug of black coffee, took it to Nick. 'Sit up. Drink that.'

178

Again Nick obeyed him, Leo took the mug back, returned it to the kitchen.

Three in the morning had struck before he left.

Nick woke to the telephone pealing angrily in his ear. He rolled over to pick it up. A thousand sledge hammers attacked his skull, while his stomach rebelled instantly, and he sweated as though he'd been in a Turkish bath. He was forced to lie still to allow the spinning world to settle. The telephone pealed on inexorably. Finally he managed to lift the receiver, bring it to his ear. He was shivering now. 'Waring,' he said faintly.

'Dr Waring? Is that you?'

'Speaking.' He was astonished. For some curious reason he'd supposed Leo to be on the line. Now why on earth should he have thought that?

'Dr Waring, Sister Carter for you.'

Sister Carter was casualty sister at Eversholt's from nine until two each day.

'Dr Waring?'

'Yes, sister,' he said wearily. 'What is it?'

The telephone grew frenzied. Dimly he made out 'after eleven, doctor, and you see I had no idea where you could be. I'm sorry to disturb you at home, but I didn't know what else to do. You do remember, don't you, that Mr Croham is coming in at midday?'

'No,' he said in a fading voice. 'No, I didn't remember, sister. What time is it now?'

'After eleven, doctor.'

After eleven? How could it be?

'And I simply didn't know *where* you'd got to.' This was not strictly accurate, of course. The switchboard had told her. 'Dr Waring went off to a dinner party in Hampstead last night. So he's probably at home, hung up, if you ask me. Shall I try ringing him there?'

'All right, sister. I'll be in.' He put the receiver back. Sat up, put his head in his hands while the room revolved and the bed turned somersaults. He had to pull himself together, somehow make it to Eversholt's inside half an hour. What the hell could have happened last night? Why did he keep thinking Leo had been here?

Somehow he succeeded in climbing to his feet, staying on them, swaying blindly through to the bathroom. He put his head in cold water until it began to clear. He tried to be sick, too, but his stomach, although so queasy, was apparently empty. What had happened to all that jugged hare?

Jugged hare. That was right. He remembered that. Jugged hare in Hampstead, at

Willie's. After that it was a blank.

He staggered into the kitchen, put on the kettle for black coffee. He must have had coffee last night, he saw. Everything was out, though the mugs were clean, draining on the side.

Leo. Black coffee.

No, it escaped him again. Why he should keep imagining he'd seen Leo last night was beyond him. The man he had to see, *stat*, was Croham. He drank two mugs of coffee, swallowed two aspirin, dressed, crept into Eversholt's. He felt at least a hundred and two, his legs were cottonwool, his stomach churned, his mouth was a bird-cage, and his head inhabited by competing road drills. He alternately shivered and sweated. His colour must have been revolting, too. Sister Carter took one look, exclaimed, 'Are you sure you're all right, doctor? Sit down here. Shall I get them to bring you a cup of tea?' She took a closer look. 'Or would you like some Ammon. aromat.?'

'No, thank you, sister.' He was terse. Sal volatile. Did she think she had a fainting teenager on her hands?

At this point Mr Croham arrived from the wards, accompanied by the orthopaedic registrar. 'Morning, Waring, morning sister.

181

Patient ready for me? Hullo, Waring, you all right?'

'Yes, thank you, sir. Just had a bit of a party last night.'

Sister Carter nodded to herself.

'Well, as long as the game's worth the candle, Waring,' Croham said, bellowing with laughter. 'If you can stand it, it's up to you, isn't it?'

'Yes, sir. Not sure I can stand it, though. There was this jugged hare. Very good indeed. And claret. Then some punch, to round the evening off. *Whew.* Seems to have been a lethal combination.' Funny, he'd forgotten the punch until this moment.

'Punch, eh? Asking for trouble, m'boy. Never accept *concoctions.*'

'No, sir. I'll remember it in future.'

'Accept my advice, Waring. Take your drinks straight always, and try and get a glimpse of the bottle, too. None of these poisonous mixtures. Only lead to trouble. Seen it again and again.'

'Yes, sir. I shan't forget.' Like hell he would. Meanwhile the roadworks continued in his head, and the demolition squad were hard at work in his belly. Sister Carter, he saw, had one wary eye on him, but he lasted out until Croham, with more hearty laughter, took himself off.

'Would you like to go and lie down in the small examination room, Dr Waring?' Sister Carter inquired solicitously. 'And I can bring you a cup of tea myself.'

He knew what that meant. 'Myself'. As you aren't fit to be seen by the staff, she was implying. Well, he couldn't afford to be proud. 'Thank you, sister.' He made it to the small examination room, went in, lay down thankfully on the couch. The room seemed to be breathing in and out with him, heaving backwards and forwards. He shut his eyes, opened them to find Sister Carter clinking a tea cup and looking almost panicky. 'Thank you, sister. That's great.' He took the tea, and the cup clattered in the saucer, while the tea slopped. Sister Carter took it back, looked even more alarmed.

'Dr Waring, are you *sure* you're all right?'

He had to laugh. 'Not precisely, sister. But I'll survive.' This time he took the tea successfully, drank it.

'Would you like some aspirin?'

'I took two when you rang.'

'That was at eleven. It's half past one now. I'll fetch you another cup of tea and a couple of more aspirin, shall I?'

'Thanks you, sister.'

She was back quickly. 'You take these, Dr Waring, and then I should have a little sleep if I were you. I'll tell Sister Bowmaker you're lying down in here, and we can call you if we need you. It's fairly quiet today so far.'

Luckily for him, it went on being quiet. He slept until nearly three, awoke clear-headed. He sat up cautiously. The room failed to revolve, the sledge hammers in his skull were a faint and distant echo only. Outside a door banged and a telephone shrilled. He didn't even wince. 'You've recovered, Waring,' he told himself sternly. 'Get on your feet and justify your existence. Maybe you do still feel a hundred and two, but you can totter out and see to things.'

Sister Bowmaker was delighted at his recovery. 'Oh, doctor, are you feeling better? I am glad. Sister Carter said you wasn't at all the thing earlier. What a pity Mr Croham had to choose today to come in – otherwise you could 'ave stayed quietly at 'ome. If only you'd thought to tell me 'ow poorly you was feeling, I'd 'ave got Tich or one of the boys to run you round 'ere in the van.'

He thanked her. 'It was only a hangover,' he said sheepishly.

'Some 'angover,' Sister Bowmaker retorted. 'Sister Carter said you was a very nasty colour, doctor. And you don't look any too good now, either. Some punch, was it?'

'That's right. On top of the jugged hare.'

'Ah well now. That accounts for it. Made-up drinks and made-up dishes. I don't 'old with neither.'

'It was very good jugged hare,' he said. It had been. But Sister Bowmaker was right. The hangover was out of all proportion. And he'd only drunk a few mouthfuls of the punch, surely? He pushed these thoughts aside. What mattered was that he'd done nothing all day. Forget the previous evening, settle down to today's needs and problems.

'Who is there to see?' he demanded.

'Only two patients from yesterday, for their dressings. Nurse is doing one of them, but I thought you'd probably like to see the other. And a little boy 'oo's ricked 'is ankle. 'Is Mum thinks 'e's broken 'is leg, of course.'

'And has he?'

Sister Bowmaker blew a raspberry, a habit of hers which had astonished him on his first arrival at Eversholt's – sisters at the Central not sharing this custom – but which he had come to accept as an expression of her unerring judgment.

'Okay, I'll see him.'

Sister Bowmaker was correct, as usual.

Not even a sprain. He reassured the child's mother – the small boy himself was perfectly happy and in need of no support at all. He looked at the stitches he'd put in the next patient. A railwayman with a gashed thumb appeared. The afternoon wound slowly on. It was a day for minor injuries. The worst case was an old lady of eight-five, who had slipped on her way to collect her pension. She was bruised and shaken, but even she appeared to have broken nothing. In view of her age, though, he admitted her, to be on the safe side. She was furious.

'Stay in ternight, young man? Whatever for? And 'oo's ter see ter puss?'

She was taken, indignant still, to the main block. He was through for the day. Escaping while Sister Bowmaker's back was turned – he had a strong suspicion she would like to admit him overnight too, just to be on the safe side – he walked slowly home to Minster Row. Now he had to recover the missing hours, find an explanation. What the hell had happened last night? Head down, deep in thought, he went down the area steps, let himself in. And as he did so, a memory flooded back. 'Key of front door.' Leo had been in a rage with him, had taken his key from him – where had they been?

He'd been sitting in Leo's car. He could remember it distinctly. Leo had taken the key, disappeared, reappeared, and then – oh God, he could hardly believe it, but it had happened, he was certain – Leo had more or less carried him down the steps, into the flat dumped him on the sofa. He had made black coffee.

Leo had cleaned him up, too. He'd been sick, he could remember that. So much for the jugged hare.

Leo must have found him somewhere, out for the count, presumably. He'd not only driven him home, seen him safely into the flat, but he must have stayed, set to and made black coffee, forced it down him, and cleaned up generally. Leo must have put him to bed, too.

No wonder he'd been in a rage.

Leo. Of all people. Nick groaned aloud.

Last night must have finished him for ever.

He put his head in his hands, shivered.

He'd been nursing a secret hope, ever since he'd left the Central, that one day he'd be able to go to Leo and explain what it was that had caused him to make such a mess of his first year as a registrar. Not that there was the slightest chance he would ever have got back to the Central, he knew that. Once you'd dropped out of the race there you'd had it. The competition was too keen. There were too many coming up behind you, prepared to fight every inch of the way. Once you'd allowed it to slip off, you'd never get your foot on the ladder again. But he had cherished this secret plan that one day he'd be able to tell Leo what had happened to him, how he'd had the problem of Louise, why he had had to put her first. With a good period of hard work behind him at Eversholt's, a reference from Croham and another from Leo, he'd thought he might be in the running for a decent job outside London.

Last night had put paid to that.

If it hadn't been for Sister Carter's loyal support, he'd have failed to meet Croham, too. Then there'd have been trouble. Croham would have found out he hadn't been in all day, hadn't even telephoned. Even Eversholt's wouldn't stand for that. As it was, thanks to Sister Carter, he'd got by. He couldn't help wondering uneasily what Croham might have said to the orthopaedic registrar as they'd walked across to the car park together.

Whatever he'd said, it would be nothing compared with what Leo must be thinking.

Nick involuntarily shut his eyes. Above all,

he had valued Leo's opinion. When he'd been his house surgeon, he'd loved every minute of the job. Not that Leo was easy to work for. He could be a devil. He demanded all you have to give, and more. Took the mickey without mercy. But his surgery was an education, and you could rely on him until hell froze.

Like last night. Wherever Leo had found him, whatever had preceded their arrival here, Leo had brought him home.

In all his twenty-six years, Nick had never experienced shame like this.

The telephone rang. He leapt on it. He expected it to be Leo.

But it was Willie.

'How are you, dear boy? I was a little worried about you.'

Worried. Nick let out a short bark of sardonic laughter. He pulled himself together hastily, apologized to Willie.

'I'm afraid it was all that punch,' Willie said. 'I should have warned you. You had rather a lot of it, I'm afraid. And after the claret, it was too much for you. I blame myself entirely.'

'All that punch?' He didn't remember drinking much. 'I don't remember drinking much punch,' he commented, puzzled.

'No, no, I daresay you don't.' Willie's voice

189

was more worried than ever. 'Oh dear, I should have stopped you.' He sounded anguished.

Dear old Willie, he really was extraordinarily kind.

'You got home all right, anyway?' Willie was continuing with his anxious inquiries. 'I was rather distressed when Perry told me he hadn't taken you there.'

'Where did he take me?' Now they might be getting somewhere. Where had Peregrine left him?

'You don't remember?' Willie's voice rose. 'Perry shouldn't have listened to you. I told him so as soon as I heard.'

'But where did he leave me?'

'You mean to say you don't remember at all?'

'I can't remember a darned thing between leaving your flat and reaching here,' Nick said bitterly.

There was a brief silence.

Nick saw he must have shocked Willie. And no wonder. He shocked himself. 'Look,' he began, 'I really am most terribly sorry, Willie. I'm afraid I behaved appallingly. I don't know what to say. Quite inexcusable, I...'

'No, no, Nick. I ought to have seen what

was happening. Considerably older and wiser, dear boy, I should have seen how things were going and stopped you much earlier.'

Nick shut his eyes again. He'd brought it all on himself. Willie had been worried to death. Nick understood only too clearly what must have happened. He'd got sloshed. He must have been knocking it back all evening. He was as bad as Louise. Drugs for her, alcohol for him. What could Willie be thinking?

'I am most fearfully sorry, Willie,' he said again. 'The trouble is, I've no memory for last night at all. I must have been much worse than I realized. A frightful nuisance to everyone. Where did Peregrine leave me? Because I think I must somehow have landed up at the Central.'

'You made Perry take you there, dear boy. Said you had to be on duty.'

Nick was unable to speak.

'I told Perry he should have paid no attention, but he said you wouldn't listen to him. You said you had to do your round, and he was afraid you'd try to get out of the car if he didn't stop.'

'My former chief brought me home,' Nick said, in doom-laden tones.

'I'm glad *someone* had the sense to take

you home, even if Perry didn't.' Willie was tart.

'Yes, but – it was my chief, Willie. You don't understand. He – I – well, I suppose my career was finished anyway, as far as the Central was concerned, but all the same – well, this has finally put paid to everything.' To unburden himself was an enormous relief, and Willie was extraordinarily kind and patient. He heard him out, his only comments small interjections of 'Oh dear', 'Poor Nick, what bad luck', 'I am so sorry, dear boy'.

When Nick had poured out the whole miserable story, Willie made an attempt to cheer him up. 'We must simply set to and see what we can do to re-establish you,' he said encouragingly. 'I feel sure if we put our heads together, we shall be able to think of something. I feel very much responsible. Anything I can do to put matters right, you can rely on me to do.'

Tremendously kind of him. But quite useless. Willie couldn't grasp the undoubted fact that there was nothing whatsoever to be done about Nick's career now. It had gone for good. Sunk without trace. All the hopes and aspirations. Wasted. Thrown away for ever. Willie meant well, though, and Nick thanked him profusely, apologized again. By his sympathetic listening alone, he had helped Nick already. 'I do feel much better now I've talked it over with you,' he told him.

Willie was touched. 'My dear Nick, anything I can do, at any time. Don't hesitate. Count on me.'

Nick thanked him again.

'We must plan a campaign. We must have a good talk. Let me see now, how about the day after tomorrow? Sunday. We'll see what Mrs Heneage can rustle up for us.'

'I've been enough of a nuisance to you already,' Nick protested.

'No, no. We must have a good talk about your future, dear boy. You come along on Sunday about half past six, say.' Willie was determined, and Nick accepted thankfully.

In Hampstead, Willie put the telephone down, rubbed his hands together. Pink and chubby, his face rosy with good humour, his eyes twinkled happily as he made a note in his diary. 'Six-thirty on Sunday,' he murmured. 'Nick.' He underlined the name, shut the book with a snap.

CHAPTER ELEVEN

LEO AND SOPHIE

Nick wanted to go and see Leo. Try to explain. Except that what had happened was beyond explanation. Or excuse. Was he looking for a shoulder to cry on? Leo would never be that.

He walked edgily about the flat. Obviously he must be considerably better, he thought dispassionately. A few hours ago he had asked only to be allowed to lie still. Now here he was, prowling the place like a caged animal.

Why expect a shoulder to cry on? He was as bad as Louise, everlastingly searching for her father-figure. Pull yourself together, Waring. You're adult, you run your own life. You don't require any shoulder to cry on, Leo's or Willie's. But an apology you do owe to Leo, in person or at least by letter.

He could ask Sophie. He'd tell her what a mess he was in, see what she thought he ought to do about Leo. He reached for the telephone. Thank God for Sophie.

She was out. Barbie answered, curt and unhelpful. 'No, I'm afraid she's not in, Nick.' She didn't say she was sorry, certainly didn't sound it. Barbie disliked him these days. He'd brought that on himself, too, he knew. 'She's having a meal with Leo, I think,' Barbie suddenly added, as he was about to ring off.

Leo and Sophie.

A new and disconcerting thought. Leo was a bachelor. He couldn't be much more than ten years older than Sophie, when you came to think about it. All these concerts and dinners together.

Sophie would do far better with Leo than with him. A leading London surgeon, Assistant Director of Surgery at the Central. Also one of the nicest of blokes. Honest. Reliable. And affectionate. Leo would make a good husband.

Was he to lose Sophie too?

He deserved to lose her. He was a failure, who could no longer blame Louise. He was a man who had had it all in front of him, but who had proved unequal to the demands life made. Now he was no more than a drunken derelict, who held down his job at Eversholt's only through the kindness and maternal care of two nursing sisters from the back streets of King's Cross.

He paced the basement flat in despair, looked at it with desperation. He expected Sophie to come here to see him. Here. Look at the place.

This was the moment at which he pulled himself up. All right, then, look at it, he said to himself. Look at it, and use your head. Stop indulging in a welter of self-pity and think.

After all, he'd never made a habit of getting drunk, having to be returned home sick and sorry by a senior surgical consultant at his teaching hospital. In eight years of medicine this had never happened before. Nor had he failed in the past to turn up on time, at Eversholt's or anywhere else. So what had happened last night? Had it been Willie's punch? Willie blamed himself, he said so.

Reconstruct the evening.

Now. He stood in the bedroom. Bed not made. Begin there, then. Make it.

Pyjamas. Leo must have put him into those. What had he been wearing before, where was yesterday's gear?

Gear. New gear to impress Sophie. Where was it?

Here. A couple of carrier bags. That's right.

He'd bought two shirts, two pairs of trousers, and a jacket. He'd thought Sophie would like the shirts, like his new image. But Sophie was out with Leo. Admiring his shirt, no doubt.

He opened the bag. One lilac shirt. Hell, there should surely be two. Where was the other, the blue one?

He'd been wearing it. That was the explanation. Leo would have put it in the laundry basket. Leo always put everything in its right place. He went into the bathroom.

Not in the laundry basket. Soaking in a polythene bucket. Meticulous Leo. Nick shuddered. What a mess he must have been in when Leo picked him up.

He'd wash the shirt out at once. Maybe he did feel a bit queasy still, but he could wash a shirt out. He ran hot water, added detergent, transferred the shirt to the basin.

Not his shirt.

He stared at it, ran it through his fingers, continued to stare blankly. He must be totally out of touch. He could remember nothing about this shirt. He'd never seen it before.

Well, here it was, so he'd better rinse it out, hang it up to dry. It was a horrible shirt. Torn. Stained.

So where was his new shirt? And his trousers?

Good grief. And his new cord jacket?

He'd seen too much of London's drop-outs and junkies not to know what had occurred. He'd been gone over. Stripped. He looked in the laundry basket, without any expectation of finding a thing, simply as a final hopeless check. But there were his trousers. He drew them out, went over them carefully. Greasy and stained, but impeccably creased. These were his new trousers all right, worn for the first time when he had left this flat yesterday. What the hell could have happened to him? Where had he been? Where had Leo found him?

He'd have to ask him. He must know. He'd have to leave it until tomorrow, but in the morning, he'd ring Leo and grovel. But ask him, too, what he needed to know. In the meantime he'd better have some food, a bath, and an early night. And try not to think about Sophie.

Far from admiring Leo's shirt, Sophie was having a battle with him. He'd been in an odd mood all day, and at lunch, when he came in to sign his letters before a clinic, he'd said abruptly, 'I wanna 'ave a word with you. But I've got this medical committee at eight. Come 'ome and 'ave a bite first?'

She had thanked him, accepted.

'We'll try to get away early,' he promised. Being Leo, he succeeded in his aim, and at half past five they left the hospital together, walked round the corner to his flat.

'We'll have a drink and then an early meal,' he suggested. 'Sit dahn and get the weight of your feet, while I 'ave a deco in the kitchen.'

Sophie knew that Leo's housekeeper, who came in daily, cooked him dishes, left them in the vast refrigerator with little notes attached. 'An hour at 400', perhaps, or even 'Three hours at 250', or 'I can finish off tomorrow'. Sophie had eaten some excellent meals on this system.

''Ow about chicken and mushrooms – stew, she must mean – with rice and tomatoes?' he yelled out. 'She says an hour in the oven for both. Means we could eat at a quarter to seven.'

'Great.'

'I'll put some 'ock on ice.'

'Lovely.'

He came back into his living room, all stainless steel, rosewood and black leather, poured drinks for them both. 'Knock that back,' he said. 'I want to talk to you. You won't like it. I'm worried about Nick Waring.'

'About Nick?' Sophie sat as upright as if

he'd passed an electric current through her.

'No need to spill your drink, fat'ead. That won't 'elp no one.' He departed to the kitchen again, returned with a clean tea towel, mopped up. 'Yes. About Nick. I found 'im in St Anne's Gardens last night. Drunk as a lord and sick as a dog.' And drugged to the eyeballs, too. But this he planned to break to her later, when she had had time to recover a little.

'Tell me about it.' She had paled. But she was in control of herself, though Leo could see her clenched hands white at the knuckles. 'When was this, anyway?'

'Last night, a bit before eleven.' Leo, as usual, was accurate. 'I was on me way back 'ere, I'd been up to the Intensive Care Unit to 'ave a last look at old Prothero.'

'And Nick was in St Anne's Gardens? What on earth was he doing there?'

'Being sick. I told you.'

'So you did.'

'And a right drop-out 'e looked, I can tell you. 'E was filthy. And very drunk. I got 'im into the car, took 'im 'ome. Gave 'im coffee, did a bit of cleaning up, got 'im to bed in the end. I think 'e'd 'ad drugs as well. Morphine type. Probably heroin, I'm afraid.' Better give it to the girl straight, get it over with.

'He can't have done.'

''E 'ad. And people 'ave been talking. You know that as well as I do. You've stuck out against the stories, gone on seeing 'im. I've been with you most of the way. Now, though, I don't know so much. They may 'ave been right all the time.'

'No, they haven't.'

'Facts, duckie, facts. Gotta face 'em.'

'Tell me exactly what happened, then.'

He told her, repeated his impression that Nick had been drugged. 'Pinpoint pupils, any'ow. And he wasn't simply drunk, either. Though 'e was that too. Pronounced smell of alcohol. And car grease.'

'Nick doesn't own a car.'

'And vomit, of course,' Leo added.

Sophie wrinkled her nose. 'He must have ponged horribly.'

'Oh, 'e did, I can tell you. But not, I noticed, of stale sweat or stale anything else. All fresh smells. But,' he was applying his first-class mind to the oddities of the episode now, 'but, you know, I'd say whatever it was 'e took, 'e'd taken very recently. And I'd also 'azzard a guess, now I come to think of it, that when 'e started out that evening 'e was reasonably presentable. Except for 'is shirt, which was filthy with the dirt of months.

Looked like the sort of shirt I keep for gettin' underneath me car.'

'Nick hasn't got a car,' Sophie repeated. Leo had said facts, and at present she was sticking to them.

'No. I reckon 'e'd been gone over pretty thoroughly at some stage. But that doesn't fit with 'im only 'aving taken 'is poison soon before I found 'im. Another oddity. 'Is flat was clean and tidy.'

'It always is. It's not a bad flat at all.'

'Could be worse. Not much, though. But I'll admit that 'owever 'orrible it was outside, inside it looked like the Nick Waring 'oo was my 'ouseman. And that don't fit, either. 'Ole situation wants looking into. But not by you. I want you to stay clear of the young idiot for a while.'

'You want me...' Leo's calm assumption of authority took Sophie's breath away. She gaped, momentarily stunned. 'Oh no,' she said, as soon as she regained the power of speech. 'I'm going straight round to see him. Now.' She stood up, looked round for her coat.

'Nah then, calm down.'

'I'm going along...'

'You're going to do nothing of the sort. Sit dahn, count ten, and start using y'r loaf. If you must go along to that 'ole and see that stoopid nit, I can't stop you. I've got me meeting at eight, and after that you're on your own, blast you. In the meantime, finish y'r drink, and remember you're 'aving supper with me.'

Sophie flushed. 'I'm sorry, Leo. Of course I'm having supper with you. Thank you very much. I'm sorry I got excited. All the same, after supper, if you don't mind, I think I'll go along and see how Nick is.' Huge green eyes stared invincibly at him from the misleadingly fragile bone structure.

'Up to you. I'd rather you didn't.'

'Why?'

'Because I don't like the prospect of you being involved in whatever's going on.'

'If Nick is, then I am.'

'I daresay, I daresay.' He eyed her speculatively.

Sophie knew that look. He was deciding how best to handle her. Well, she wasn't going to be handled.

The oven-timer began to cluck imperiously from the kitchen. Leo went out, reappeared with a casserole and hot plates. 'Any'ow,' he said comfortably, 'we'll eat, then we can decide what you're going to do while we 'ave our coffee.'

'I'm not...'

'And I'm not 'aving me food spoiled by a load of argument. So pipe down. And sit down, too.' He returned to the kitchen, while Sophie obediently sat down at the circle of rosewood and steel that was Leo's dining table. He returned with the hock, poured it into heavy cut glass.

Sophie sipped it. 'Heavenly, Leo.' Ice-cold and dry, a faint, fascinating flavour that lingered. And it was more than time that she began to express some appreciation, instead of a stream of obstinate disagreement with everything he uttered. 'I don't know where you get it, or what you pay, but it's heaven, Leo. I should think you must pay the earth. My father would say you can taste the grape.' It had dawned on her, too, that whatever Leo might say about Nick, he had looked after him and taken him home last night.

Leo, who did pay the earth, was pleased. 'Yeah. I think it's good,' he agreed, and drank. 'You serve the casserole. Reckon I've done enough.'

Sophie lifted the lid off the gold Worcester ovenware. Savoury steam poured out.

'Ah ha,' Leo said, with a gleam of anticipation. 'Starvation camp. It's what *my* father used to say,' he added, seeing her blankness, 'whenever we 'ad anything extra tasty.'

'Starvation camp,' Sophie repeated. She liked the phrase, could easily imagine a family of fat cheerful Rosensteins sitting round, consuming huge steaming platefuls.

Over coffee, Leo opened his campaign in a low key. 'Now, about Nick. Must say, I don't care for the look of it.'

'Neither do I.' Sophie was distinctly snappish. 'Who could?'

'No. I'd still like you to stay out of it, though.'

'You know what I think about that.'

'I'll make you a proposition.' He might have been in the market at Leather Lane.

'A proposition?'

'Yeah. Stay out of it and I'll go and 'ave a talk to 'im meself.'

There was nothing wrong with Sophie's mind. She took in the full implication of Leo's offer instantly. 'When?' she asked.

'Stone the crows, girl, I dunno when. When I 'ave time. In the next few days.'

'Tomorrow.'

Leo eyed her. 'If I do, you'll keep out?' He was suspicious. He had expected more argument than this.

'If you go and see Nick tomorrow, I'll wait

until I hear from you before getting in touch with him.' Sophie was righteous.

Leo had known there was a catch in it. 'And then you'll still say you don't agree with me, and you're off to see for yourself, I suppose?'

'Probably.'

'Not good enough.' Leo shrugged, back in Leather Lane. 'Don't think I'll bovver. Why should I waste me time? Going to be no stopping you. I wash me 'ands.' He shrugged again, watched Sophie belligerently. He didn't even bother to pretend, Sophie thought. This was by no means his final offer. But he had taken up a strong position. Trust Leo. His intervention was too vital to be thrown away, and, blast him, he knew it. He was simply bullying her.

Sophie capitulated. 'What do you want me to do, then?' she asked.

Leo had won. 'Stay away until I tell you.'

'All right. As long as you're in touch with him. I won't be.'

A worthy adversary. Leo saw himself inescapably committed to more than one fleeting visit of inspection. Sophie had made plans for him to hold a watching brief. He grinned amiably. 'I'll see 'im and form an opinion' was all he said.

'Thank you, Leo.'

'Now I must go. This meeting – have I got the papers?'

'In your brief-case.'

He rummaged. 'Yeah, I see.' His eye travelled down the agenda. 'Right, let's go.'

They went down in the lift together, then separated. Sophie walked slowly home to St Anne's Square, not knowing what to think. Nick was in some trouble that she didn't understand. On the other hand, Leo was going to investigate it.

Leo's committee finished early, and he found himself wondering about Nick. So he set off for Minster Row, parked the Jaguar behind Tich Bowmaker's van, rang the bell.

Nick, on his way to bed, was astonished to hear the bell. Could it possibly be Sophie? In dressing gown and pyjamas, he went to the door. Leo. His jaw dropped.

'You look a bit better than you did this morning,' Leo remarked. 'Though not much.'

'Yes, sir. I feel a good deal better, thank you.' Leo walked in, Nick followed him into the sitting room. 'I – I was going to ring you in the morning,' he said. 'I – to – well, to thank you, and – I mean...' He found he couldn't meet Leo's eyes. 'I'm extremely sorry, sir. About it all.'

'So I should 'ope,' Leo said unhelpfully.

Nick began to make the fire up. It gave him something to do with his hands, allowed him to turn his back, too, while his thoughts whirled wildly. Why had Leo come? To see if he was all right? Or to tick him off? Or what?

Of course. He'd been having dinner with Sophie. She had sent him. He'd have told her about last night, she'd have been worried. 'Did Sophie send you along?'

The inquiry amused Leo. He thought Nick had considerable nerve to catechize him at all, though it was like him to leap unerringly to the correct conclusion. 'More or less,' he agreed. He thought of Sophie, almost out-manoeuvring him. Now here was young Nick interrogating him. Together they formed quite a team, he had to admit.

'She shouldn't have asked you,' Nick was saying. 'However, I would have been on to you in the morning myself. I wanted to find out what was going on last night.'

'If you take drugs you must expect that sort of trouble,' Leo said curtly.

'Drugs?'

'That's what I said.' Leo was hoping Nick wasn't going to start lying to him. If so, he was through with him.

208

'Drugs?' Nick said again. He pushed his sleeve up, rubbed a reddened patch on his arm thoughtfully, extended his arm wordlessly.

Leo came over and peered at it. 'Yes.'

'I found it ten minutes ago, while I was having a bath. I was only just beginning to wonder about it.' He broke off. 'Will you sit down, sir? Can I get you anything? Only coffee or tea, I'm afraid.'

Leo sat down in front of the now flickering fire. 'Nothing, thanks. Simply tell me what the 'ell's going on. That's what I came to see you about.'

'I wish I knew.' Nick stared at his arm again. 'Until ten minutes ago I assumed I'd had one hell of a hangover. I was going to apologize to you, never drink punch again, and put it down to experience. Or try to. But for the last few minutes I haven't been sure. I know it's a bit much, but may I ask you some questions?'

'Go ahead.'

'What time did you find me, and where?'

'Ten forty-five. St Anne's Gardens.'

'*Ten forty-five?* But I can't have left Hampstead before ten-fifteen.'

'You were drugged when I found you, I'm fairly certain,' Leo told him. 'You were also very sick.'

'I know. I'm sorry. My clothes are lost, too.'

'Lost?'

'A corduroy jacket and a shirt. I thought I'd been out for several hours somewhere, and they'd been taken off me then. But if you found me at ten forty-five, there wasn't much time to strip me. It's extraordinary.' He frowned, rubbed his hand through his already rumpled dark hair, looking very young indeed.

Leo took a chance. He thought this was too muddled and honest an account to be a lie. Unless Waring had totally lost contact with reality, he was giving him the truth. 'If you're sure you left Hampstead at ten-fifteen, and I'm certain I found you outside the Central at ten forty-five, there simply wasn't enough time for you to be roaming around drunk and getting into that amount of trouble. Let's go over your time-table, make sure you haven't mislaid an hour somewhere.'

Nick recounted his evening from leaving Eversholt's at five-thirty until Willie looked at his little gilt clock and announced it was time for the punch.

'That was nine-thirty. He said so, and I

could see it was. Then he and Louise fussed about, fetching a bowl, and the ingredients, and a little spirit stove – all very olde worlde, it was – glasses and spoons, a ladle, simply tremendous paraphernalia. He poured stuff out, heated it, put this and that in, tasted it himself at intervals. He's the one who ought to have been knocked out by it, now I come to think of it. Anyway, he can't possibly have had it ready in less than twenty minutes, more like half an hour. In fact, I believe his little clock chimed again. He gave a glass to Peregrine, and I had the second glass. Now I'd have sworn you know, that I had at the most a few sips of the stuff. But Willie says I drank quarts of the brew. I can only assume that it must have gone to my head at once, and I didn't notice after that how much I was drinking. But my impression remains the same – that I drank very little of it, a mouthful or two, and the room started spinning.' He produced an ironical and deprecating smile. 'Typical alcoholic's so-called confession, I'm afraid.'

'Could be. Or could be this Willie fellow handed you a Mickey Finn.'

'A Mickey Finn? A knock-out dose? In the punch? Willie? But why on earth should he do that?'

'Can't imagine. You tell me.'

'He's a dear old boy.'

'On what do you base this impression?' Leo might have been examining for the Fellowship.

'Superficial impressions, mostly, I suppose,' Nick had to admit. 'But he's taken my sister up, seems to be making something of her. Which is more than I could do.'

'Why did he take your sister up?'

Nick shook his head. 'Don't know, if it wasn't simple kindness. And because Peregrine asked him to, of course. Now, if you'd suggested that Peregrine had handed me a Mickey Finn, I'd believe you. Though even then, I can't see what for, what he hoped to gain.'

'I think you'd better tell me 'oo all these people are. But first I'd like that cuppa you mentioned earlier.'

Nick could have thrown his arms round the corpulent figure of his former chief, and cried like a child. He'd wanted a shoulder to cry on. He'd got one. Leo was taking enormous trouble. And when Leo took trouble there were results.

He owed it to Sophie, of course. Sophie had nagged Leo into it.

In default of bursting into tears, Nick went

briskly into the kitchen and made tea. He and Leo sat over it, talking in front of the fire late into the night.

CHAPTER TWELVE

THE WHITE POPPY

Leo put his foot down about Sophie. 'Want to talk about Soph now,' he'd said, before he left.

Nick had gone still. 'Yes?'

'I don't want you to let 'er involve 'erself in this. Whatever this is. There's something going on, and I think she ought to be kep' aht of it. But she'll come pokin' 'er nose in, you wait and see.'

'No, she mustn't. It's too dicey.'

'If you can stop 'er, young Nick, you're a better man than I am. But I don't think she ought to come to this flat. Not no more.'

'No. No, she mustn't.' He knew Leo was right. 'I'll tell her not to.'

Leo grinned. 'I told 'er not to earlier this evening. It 'ad not the faintest effect.'

'I notice she didn't actually get here, sir.' Nick's eyes danced. Leo's support had had the most elevating effect on his spirits.

'You'd better come along to my place, 'ave

a bite, termorrer evening. We'll get 'er along, and we'll both talk to 'er like Dutch uncles.'

So two improbable Dutch uncles, one short and fat, the other tall and lean, received Sophie, who came swirling in wearing a coat Nick hadn't seen before, a great tawny fox fur. A wisp of a girl, lost in a vast coat, her great green eyes peered out from the billowing fur, a massive fox hat drowned her hair. She looked fragile and very desirable. Her sophistication momentarily took Nick's breath away, but she flew straight into his arms, and it was the same Sophie inside the flummery. He held her tightly.

'Very affecting,' Leo commented. 'I'll see if I can find us anything to eat.' He stumped off to the kitchen. It was his version of tact and discretion.

'There's a mass to tell you,' Nick began, when he had divested Sophie of the coat, and they were sitting together on Leo's great black leather chesterfield. 'It's all rather weird.'

'What in the world had happened to you when Leo ran into you?'

'If it wasn't for him I wouldn't have the faintest idea. He's more or less worked it out for me, but it's still a bit incredible.' He told her some of Leo's conclusions.

He joined them, began pouring drinks. 'You 'eard?' he inquired over his shoulder.

'I don't like it at all,' Sophie said.

Nick smiled at her. Nothing bothered him now. 'Nor did I, at the time,' he said. 'However, one point. You mustn't come to the flat any more. Or to Eversholt's. Not down there at all. It's too worrying. I can't be looking after you and Louise, wondering what the hell you're both up to, where you've got to. I'll ring you, and that's that.'

Looking at Nick, her eyes wide, she took it like a lamb. 'All right,' she said soberly.

Nick regarded her alertly. So did Leo. Neither of them trusted the easy walk-over.

'I mean it,' Nick said suspiciously.

'I can see you do. I've said all right.'

'As long as you understand.'

'Of course I understand. Only too well. I wish I didn't. I don't like it. But you needn't worry about me. I won't complicate it for you.'

Nick looked at Leo, who shook his head. 'I dunno,' he admitted. 'Search me.'

'What we ought to be thinking about,' Sophie pointed out, 'isn't what I'm going to do or not do, but what Nick's going to do. Tomorrow. At Willie's. I suppose you're still set on going there? Anything might happen.'

For the first time, they both realized she was very frightened.

'I think 'e'll be all right,' Leo said. 'I don't think anything is going to 'appen. Except 'e may proposition 'im.'

'Proposition him?' Sophie was puzzled. 'What about?'

'Drugs. I think that's what all this may 'ave been about. It seems to me they've got some job they'd like 'im to undertake for 'em. Last Thursday was for the purpose of discrediting 'im. So that no one would pay no attention, you see, if 'e did 'appen to turn their offer down, start blabbing. 'Oo'd believe a word 'e said? A dropped-out drug addict.'

'But what in the world are they going to ask me to do? What is there I can do? One inoffensive junior hospital doctor. What the hell do they think they need me for?'

'I wish I knew, mate. But doctors aren't so easily come by. That's probably why they've latched on to you.'

'I still don't understand it.'

'Bent doctors are in short supply, and they think they can bend you. Of course, you and I know you're about the most unbendable creature on two legs living today. Apparently they 'aven't stumbled to this elementary fact. And that's where I've some advice.

Don't let them stumble on it. Because that might be quite dangerous.'

'You think so?' Nick couldn't prevent scepticism creeping into his voice. What was all this nonsense they'd dreamed up?

'I think it could be dangerous. No more. Don't wish to be alarmist, but we know so little, and I'd rather you didn't take chances. So if 'e does make an offer, 'owever illegal or unsavoury it may be, don't turn it down out of 'and. Say you'll 'ave to make arrangements to get away, or take time off. Anything. But don't on any account say you wouldn't touch 'is stinking job with a ten-foot pole.'

Before he saw Willie, though, Nick had a visit from Peregrine and Louise. He was on his own in the flat, reading *A Short Practice of Surgery* on Sunday morning, when they arrived. They came down the area steps, rang the bell, poured into the basement like an invading army from another world – both of them in ankle-length embroidered sheepskin coats. Peregrine's was yellow and dripped dark fur at wrists, neck and down the front opening, while Louise's, white, cascaded with white strands everywhere. Beneath it she was displaying yards of purple crochet.

They had come, they informed him, because they wouldn't see him that evening.

They were just off to Hampshire, to the motor museum at Beaulieu. Louise was to be photographed among the vintage cars, she told Nick delightedly, in Edwardian dress. She swirled about his room expatiating on the gorgeousness of the garments she would be wearing, then began commenting disparagingly on the flat. 'You've got the furniture out of store. I didn't know you were going to do that. I must say, Nickie darling, I do think you could have found a better place to put it. This is a *slum.*'

'It does me all right,' he said briefly. Today he found her exceptionally irritating, as maddening as only a relative can be. She'd destroyed his morning's reading, too.

'I must say, Nick, it is almost as sordid as that Chalk Farm horror.' Peregrine backed her up. 'Quite as sordid, to be honest, except that your own furniture is a slight improvement. But even that's a bit on the dreary side, isn't it?'

'I like it.' Nick was furious with both of them.

'My dear Nick, your taste.' Peregrine shuddered. 'However, if it suits you.' He examined him as if he had crawled from under the stove.

'But the noise, Nickie. How can you possibly stand it?' Louise shrieked at him.

'Used to it.'

She shook her head. 'Rather you than me. I simply don't know how you can.' She began walking round the room, twitching the curtains, straightening the furniture, moving oddments on his desk. Louise had always been a fidget. She couldn't keep a flat clean or tidy, but she was everlastingly moving stuff about. Now she picked up his bowl of fruit, took it away from the coffee table by the sofa, tried it on the gate-legged table in the window. 'Yes, that's better,' she told him, head on one side admiring her achievement.

'Not better for me,' Nick retorted ungratefully. 'I want to be able to reach out for an apple. From here. Bring it back, Lulu, there's a good girl.' He was sprawling on the big sofa, watching her make her tour.

'Oh Nickie, you simply have no aesthetic sense whatever. *Look* at this place.'

Peregrine came and sat down on the other end of the sofa. He had thrown his sheepskin coat over a chair, and could be viewed in the full glory of wide maroon velvet trousers, lurid appliqués dotted here and there, black shirt with full sleeves and open neck, a tank top in yellows and greens. With his hands wound round his maroon velvet knees, he scrutinized Nick.

Nick avoided his glance. He didn't want to give away his suspicions. Louise had drifted out of the room, was presumably busy shifting stuff about in the bedroom or kitchen.

'Nick, do you have to stay in this hole?' Peregrine demanded.

Nick shrugged. 'Suits me.' Was Peregrine on heroin himself, or was he a pusher? Physically free of dependence on drugs, making money out of human misery?

'Surely you could afford...' Peregrine began.

There was a sudden screech from the bedroom. 'Perry, here's your old shirt that you keep in the car. What on earth is it doing here?' Louise came round the door, the shirt in her hands. Nick had left it on the back of a chair. It puzzled him, and he had not wanted to throw it out.

Well, he was no longer puzzled. But he did his best to look as if he was.

Louise was waving it under Peregrine's nose.

He, Nick was delighted to see, had gone a nasty shade of green, very much the colour of his tank top. 'My shirt, Lulu?' he squeaked. 'Let me see. Is it? Give it to me. It can't be mine, can it?'

'But of course it is. Look. You must remember it.'

'Is it yours, Peregrine?' Nick took a hand. 'Let me see.' He reached for it, opened it out. 'Certainly doesn't look like one of mine, I must say. I don't know. Hardly looks like one of yours, either, does it?' He tried to look confused, disorientated. 'Seems to me I've seen it before, though. Where did you say you found it, Louise?'

'In your bedroom, silly. On a chair. Surely you knew it was there?'

Nick yawned. 'Can't say I did.'

'You must have done.'

'Oh Lulu, don't be daft. I don't keep track of my shirts. I just go on wearing them until I run out, then I take them down to the launderette and start again.' He hoped she'd fall for this unlikely tale. Sophie would have raised her eyebrows. Nick had a place for everything, was systematic to a fault, and couldn't have lost track of a tin tack or an elastic band if he'd tried, she had told him.

'Oh Nickie, you are the most fantastically vague creature.'

'You haven't been wearing this old thing, have you?' Peregrine inquired. He was a better colour now, had evidently decided to acknowledge the shirt.

'Don't know. Should think I must have. Can't really say.'

'But Nick...' Louise began.

'It's an old shirt I used to use in the car. To wipe my hands, that sort of thing,' Peregrine explained.

'You'd better have it back,' Nick offered, forcing himself to sound disinterested, though he had a struggle to keep the triumph out of his voice. He would have liked, too, to demand his own shirt back, his cord jacket too, show Peregrine he was on to him.

Fortunately for both of them, Louise was bored by now. She threw the shirt down on the floor. 'For heaven's sake,' she protested, 'all this fuss about that grotty old object. Can't we talk about something interesting, for a change?'

Peregrine climbed to his feet, casually retrieved the shirt. 'Time we were on our way,' he said, reaching for his coat. 'We dropped in for a moment because Lulu wanted to see your pad – and to tell you we'd be away next week, too.'

'I'm going to look super, aren't I, Perry? I shall be wearing Edwardian dresses and hats – you know, those *creations*. Put my hair up on top of my head, like this.' She scrambled it up in two hands, and gazed at him, large-eyed and seductive. Extraordinary, he thought, not for the first time, how beautiful Louise could be. One moment uninspired chaos, the next a dream of a girl. He saw why Peregrine photographed her so often, in spite of her erratic behaviour and her constant demands.

'Come along, Lulu,' he said now, and like an oddly-attired nannie in embroidered sheepskin he herded her back up the area steps and into the Citroën. 'See you on our return, Nick,' he said as he went round to the driving seat.

They drove off, Louise waving wildly and blowing extravagant kisses, like an actress on a publicity stunt.

That evening Nick found Willie alone. He greeted Nick with tremendous friendliness. 'I am glad to see you. I was really rather worried about you.'

'I was worried about myself,' Nick said. 'But I'm fully recovered. I'm afraid I simply had too much to drink.' This was the line he and Leo had agreed on. 'Stick to the truth as far as possible,' Leo had told him. 'Be yourself. It shouldn't be difficult. You only 'ave to cast your mind back, recapture your feelings when you believed what Willie told you. Be depressed, fed up, lay it on thick, so that he comes across with whatever it is 'e as in 'is mind. But don't invent.'

'I feel very much responsible,' Willie was saying. He looked sad, shook his head. 'Dear, dear. If only I had noticed what was happening. I am so sorry about it. You have had bad luck.'

'Never seem to meet anything else but bad luck.' Nick sounded petulant.

'We must see what we can do to improve the situation. You still have your post at your present hospital – Eversholt's, didn't you say?'

'That crumby dump.'

'I'm afraid I'm not familiar with the different hospitals. This one you're at now, it's a poor specimen, is it? Not like the previous one?'

'The Central was my teaching hospital. Eversholt's is a hole in the ground. By the railway. Ought to be closed down – in fact several attempts have been made to close it, so I suppose I'll be out of a job again soon.' Poor old Eversholt's. Until he heard himself running it down, he had no idea how attached to it he'd become. It wasn't a bad sort of place. 'I wouldn't go near it,' he told Willie, 'except that I have to live, pay the rent. So I try to stick it out.'

'I may be able to put you in line for a certain amount of private practice, if that would interest you at all,' Willie suggested.

Nick opened his mouth to babble enthusiastically, but Willie raised his plump little hand. 'One moment, Nick, one moment. It may not be at all the type of work that appeals to you.'

'Any work that pays real money appeals to me,' Nick assured him.

'Louise has always told me that you were interested only in surgery. Otherwise I would have mentioned this possibility before.'

'Louise doesn't understand,' Nick said impatiently. That at least was true. 'It isn't any longer a question of what I want, simply of what I can get. The Central's finished with me. Even Eversholt's may not want me, not after Friday's exhibition.' He frowned, pushed his hands through his hair, told Willie how on Friday morning he'd had to be summoned by telephone from home, had only just managed to reach the hospital before his chief, how his appearance had been commented on, and, finally, how he slept most of the afternoon in a small room off the waiting hall. He laid it on thick, as

226

Leo had advised, made it sound disastrous. It easily could have been. 'I don't know,' he ended. 'I seem to have made a total mess of my life. No good trying to kid myself any longer.' He picked up his empty sherry glass, looked into it, rudely helped himself to more, then wondered if he was hopelessly overplaying his role.

Apparently not. 'You mustn't give in like this,' Willie said firmly, adding 'I think we should have our meal now. Mrs Heneage is having one of her rare Sundays off, but she has left everything ready.' Taking the decanter with him, he disappeared into the kitchen.

Throughout the excellent dinner that followed, he remained the kindly and concerned proxy uncle, so that Nick's first doubts returned. It was Leo's theory that Willie himself must be deeply involved in whatever was going on. But Leo had never met him, after all. Was it possible that Willie's whole attitude could be an act? Nick became increasingly doubtful. Willie was a dear old man, worried about a drunken young wastrel of a doctor, slipping into alcoholism and living in a slum.

At last Willie returned to his original suggestion. Private practice, he said. People he knew would be only too glad to be able to call upon the services of a young and up-to-date doctor, if he was prepared to hold himself available.

'What for?'

'The pay would be quite an improvement on what you receive now. And there might be some travelling, too. Weekends in the south of France sometimes, or Deauville, for example.'

Hardly an answer to his question. However, Nick said only, 'Deauville sounds great. A casino, isn't there? And I could do with some real money, for a change.'

'I'm sure you could,' Willie was sympathetic. 'It's quite scandalous, the amount the health service offers. And it can't be very pleasant, living in that basement. Private practice will set you on your feet again. I must make inquiries to see if I can't find you a more suitable flat.'

Nick was beginning to think Willie's offer genuine. Some hypochondriacal elderly friends of his, wealthy, who wanted a young doctor constantly on call, ready to pop off to the south of France or anywhere else the instant they experienced a twinge. He could guess what the snag would be, but that was hardly Willie's fault. 'I ought to warn you,' he felt compelled to say, 'that I'm only a very junior hospital doctor, without much experience. No higher qualifications. I don't know if...'

'You must try to have more confidence in yourself,' Willie interrupted him. 'Be more positive about your own achievements and capabilities.'

He had a point there, Nick knew.

'I'm quite sure you'd be competent to take on this job in Deauville. I'm told it's very simple. A French doctor goes there at present, and he tells me that all that's necessary is a straightforward laboratory technique.'

'If it's as simple as that, why send me out there? Why can't this Frenchman carry on?'

'He doesn't want to,' Willie said shortly.

'But surely you can find another Frenchman? Instead of sending someone over specially?' What could it be? Tests of some sort, presumably.

'Tell me, dear boy,' Willie was nettled, 'do you make it a habit to talk yourself out of any lucrative appointment that may by good fortune be offered to you? Because if so, it is hardly surprising, is it, that your career has failed to prosper?'

'It's just that I didn't want you to...'

'Allow me to be the judge of whether we need you or not. Now tell me, yes or no,

229

would you be available to go to Deauville for me one week-end?'

So it was 'for me' now. 'If you think I'd be able to carry out your requirements, yes, of course. I'd be glad to. But I honestly must have some idea of what I'd be asked to do first, Willie. What sort of laboratory work?'

'I'd see that you were properly informed before you went over, of course.' Willie was a little testy. 'I can't go into it all now, dear boy. In any case, I don't understand it myself. But the pay will be excellent, I can tell you that. You might have to go at short notice, of course. We'd arrange the hotel booking for you in Deauville, and there'd be a chance to visit the casino while you were there, I feel sure. So will you take it on?'

Nick still lacked the faintest notion of what they could be up to. But to press Willie further now was clearly unwise. 'Of course. It's a wonderful opportunity, Willie. Thank you for it. I might need a day or two to arrange time off from Eversholt's, that's the only problem. Can't afford to leave there.'

'We must think about that. I'm sure I can see that you're kept busy with private practice.' He began to explain what he had in mind, though at first Nick found it impossible to disentangle fact from a maze of make-believe. There was talk about south coast towns, cathedral cities, charming countryside, the downs, sea air, even opportunities for recreation. He would need a car to get about, of course, Willie said. Large secondary schools came into it, comprehensives too. At first it sounded like nothing more than the school health service.

At last, though, the picture became hideously clear. This was what Leo had foreseen. Nick's original suspicions had been correct, too. Exactly as he had feared, Peregrine was pushing drugs. This was what he engaged in when he disappeared on photographic sessions with Louise. But on a far bigger scale than anything Nick had envisaged in his worst nightmares. Supplies came in regularly, Willie finally told him, and were then distributed by Peregrine in Kent, Sussex and Hampshire. Supplies of heroin and marihuana from abroad, other drugs from centres in England. Stolen, no doubt. But where did the heroin and marihuana come from?

Of course, from Deauville and the south of France. He grasped at that point what the 'simple laboratory technique' must be, that Willie had refused to divulge. The conversion of morphine into heroin. Nick shivered.

Acid, barbiturates and amphetamines were also put out through his network, Willie was explaining. Now Nick understood. This was what they needed a doctor for. To write prescriptions when supplies were low, and do the dispensing of the stolen drugs. This was what Willie meant by private practice. Very private. And it was true they didn't need a doctor with experience or seniority. A medical student could have handled it, apart from signing the prescriptions. For that you needed to be on the medical register. But how long would he be likely to remain on it, Nick wondered?

Then he saw the entire plan. To get him off the register would take several years. Say a year or eighteen months before the prescriptions he issued became enough of a scandal for anyone to instigate action against him, and about the same period before they could in fact put a stop to his activities. About three years in all. By then, Willie and Peregrine would have made their pile and retired. Nick Waring would be on the scrap heap, if not facing a prison sentence.

And Louise? What would happen to her?

'What about Louise?' he asked.

'Oh, Louise has been of the greatest assist- ance throughout, I must say.' Willie evidently supposed Nick would be heartened by this information. 'It was she, of course, who was able to put us in touch with our supplier. And she's since been most useful to Peregrine on the distribution side, too.'

Nick felt sicker than ever. If Leo hadn't briefed him, he would have exploded into anger, have threatened to blow the entire operation sky high. And then what would have happened to him? He remembered Paul's original warning, hardly needed to guess what the next stage would be. He'd be found dead from an overdose of heroin. And no one would be surprised. No one at all.

His stunned silence was misconstrued by Willie. 'Of course,' he said, 'you have your own source of supply at present, I gather. When you leave Eversholt's, though, I'd see that you received whatever you needed.'

It was at this point that Nick saw it all. Willie and Peregrine genuinely believed him to be an addict. Louise must have told them he was. That was why they thought they could buy him. What could he say now?

'It's not easy to get hold of morphia in any form,' he said slowly, feeling his way. A true statement. Willie received it, though, as an addict's complaint.

'I know it's difficult for you now, Nick. But

we could remedy that easily. Yes, indeed. I'd see you never went short, I assure you. You would be doing a great deal of good to these young people, too, if you took this on. They need medical supervision, after all. This you could give them, couldn't you? As you dispense their prescriptions, don't you see?' Willie beamed, a benevolent Father Christmas. He was still chatting optimistically as he saw Nick out of the flat, down the stairs to the street. 'I'll let you know about Deauville in the next week or two,' he said. 'Come and see me again soon, dear boy – and always feel free to turn to me, in any difficulty you may encounter. Rely on me.'

As soon as he reached Minster Row Nick rang Leo. 'You were right,' he said. 'Drugs is what it was all about.' He explained exactly what Willie had wanted him to do.

'Stone the crows. You need the law, Nick, *stat.*'

'I thought I'd get on to Paul Worsley. He'll know the right people to contact.'

'Yeah, that would be one way. But I'm not sure I don't think you ought to 'ave a solicitor be'ind you right from the start. 'Old y're 'orses, Nick, until I've 'ad a word with me own solicitor. I'll be on to 'im first thing in the morning. Then I'll give you a ring, let you know what 'e suggests.'

What Morris Geldart suggested was that Nick should come and see him, and on Monday afternoon Nick went down to Gray's Inn, leaving one of the registrars covering the final couple of hours in casualty for him.

Morris Geldart, it appeared, had been at school with Leo – who, contrary to Central mythology, had not been to a slum school in Stepney, but to the City of London School on the embankment at Blackfriars. Geldart was a quiet slim man with glasses, almost academic, and physically about as unlike Leo as it was possible to be. He proved, however, to share many of his characteristics, including a rapid grasp of essentials and an ability to cut corners where necessary. He listened to Nick's account of Willie's proposal, asked a number of pertinent questions, extracted from him additional details about Louise and their family history, and nodded. 'You're quite right, all this will have to be reported to the drug people at the Yard. I'm glad you came to me first, though. We can make an appointment for you from here. You'll find...' his hand was already on the telephone, when it rang. 'Yes? One minute.' He looked at Nick. 'For you,' he said. 'A

Sister Bowmaker.'

Nick took the telephone. 'Yes, sister?'

'Dr Waring, the police have been on. They're trying to get hold of you, and they say it's urgent. About your sister.'

CHAPTER THIRTEEN

ARRESTS IN HAMPSTEAD

In the hall of the clinic in Berkshire, wearing the long white sheepskin coat she'd had on when she had called to see him in Minster Row only two days earlier, but pallid and haggard where before she had been vivid, excited, swirling round his room, blowing kisses as she left, Louise wept bitterly.

Nick left her there, drove back to London, exhausted after a sleepless night, discouraged, nearly in despair. Only the thought of Sophie waiting for him held comfort.

Louise, with Peregrine and Willie, had been arrested at the Hampstead flat the previous afternoon. All three of them had been taken to the police station on Haverstock Hill where Louise, in a panic, had called loudly, insistently, for Nick.

Morris Geldart had gone straight over there from Gray's Inn with him. As a result of their united efforts, the following morning, while Peregrine and Willie had been remanded in custody, Louise had been released on bail, subject to the condition that she received medical treatment. After the formalities had been completed Nick drove her – in Leo's Jaguar, loaned for the occasion – down to the clinic where she had been treated previously.

Throughout the journey she complained miserably, apparently under the impression that if only he had not stepped in, arranged for her admission to the clinic, she would by now have been installed in Willie's flat again, the clock safely turned back, all problems evaporated. 'I was happy there, Nickie. I've never been so happy,' she wailed.

He knew it was true.

'Now everything's awful. Why did you have to interfere? You don't understand. It's no good me going to this place. I can't stand it. I was perfectly all right at Willie's.'

The outlook for her was bleak, the only glimmer of hope the fact that, much as she hated it, she was under treatment again. But in a few months' time she'd come up for trial. There was no getting away from it, she was known to have been smuggling heroin into the country, passing it on to schoolchildren. Yet Nick could hardly find it in himself to hold her responsible for her actions. Those he blamed were the pushers who had first made her into an addict, though the trouble went much further back than that. Back to Trish, who had brought her into the world without caring. Now Louise was caught in a trap. Unable to escape from it unaided, rejecting all help, she was a lost girl.

He went to Leo's flat to return the Jaguar, found Morris Geldart there already, Sophie too. It was she who came to the front door to let him in, and he put his arms round her, kissed as though they'd been separated for months. For one brief moment of longing he thought of running away from it all with her. He could take Sophie home with him to the basement in Minster Row. There, undisturbed, lose himself in her beauty, her soft comforting warmth. Abandon Louise, forget Morris Geldart and Leo. Be alone with Sophie.

Instead they went together into Leo's living room, black leather, rosewood, stainless steel and glass shelving – so totally different, he thought suddenly from Willie's room with its little tables, lustres on the Adam chimneypiece, plump upholstery and damask. Morris Geldart was talking about Willie. 'He overreached himself, that's what it amounts to,' he said. 'He's been known to police and

Customs for years as a smuggler of antiques. More fraud than direct action. False invoices, goods dispatched by devious routes, that type of arrangement. Mind you, while some of his antiques seem to have been bought legitimately at sales, others had undoubtedly been stolen. But Willie Hampson managed to keep discreetly in the background, and the police told me they never laid their hands on enough evidence to bring him to court. Until now.'

'What about Peregrine?' Nick asked.

'He did the leg work in the antique fiddles. Went round taking a load of photographs in country houses which afterwards got burgled, too. Made quite a pattern, I'm told. Again, no evidence. But it was only with the arrival of your sister that the two of them moved over into drugs, and their trouble here was that they were amateurs. Right out of their depth, if you ask me. They made mistake after mistake – the approach to you, for instance. Then, instead of bringing the stuff into London and selling it to wholesalers, keeping out of distribution themselves – oh no, they were greedy, wanted a double profit, and made themselves obvious by building up their own network of pushers. That alerted the police, who soon noticed more drugs were circulating, as well as antagonizing other drug rings. Unpopular all round.' He raised his eyebrows. 'In any case,' he added, 'I ask you, how could anyone fail to spot those two, Peregrine and your sister, dancing round the depths of Hampshire in ankle-length sheepskin?' Like Leo, Morris Geldart – thin-faced with heavy horn-rimmed glasses, dark formal suit – was essentially an urban product, apt to assume impenetrable jungle began at the Chiswick fly-over. 'The outcome was a foregone conclusion. The police had just about had enough of Willie Hampson & Co. They've been watching them for months. And this week-end they were ready to act. Your sister and Peregrine...'

'What a name, blimey,' Leo interrupted. 'Bet 'e was christened George.'

'No, Percival. Well, on Sunday they were followed from the moment they left the studio in Chelsea. They arrived in Beaulieu all right, had lunch there, and took photographs that afternoon. So far so good. Then they went on to Southampton, and here, to no one's surprise, they made for the docks. By now they were being very closely tailed, of course. They met two *au pair* girls off the boat from Le Havre. These poor stupid kids were returning to their English families after a visit to their parents in France, thought they could make a little extra cash by carrying an additional case each – someone at the railways station on the other side asked them to, apparently, promised them a fat fee if they did. Peregrine and Louise met them, they all went off and had coffee together. Then the two girls set off for the London train with only one case apiece again, while Peregrine and Louise retuned to the Citroën, also carrying a case each. Peregrine paid the French girls well, and that was that. Easy money, they thought, until the police scooped them off the London train for questioning.'

'Need their heads examining if you ask me,' Leo commented, 'would you carry an extra case, Soph, if someone came up to you at Victoria or Waterloo, offered big money?' He snorted.

'I'd run a mile,' Sophie agreed.

'So would any sane human being. Don't tell me those two didn't suspect what they were being asked to do. They can't have been that dim.'

'I gather they did, but supposed they'd be carrying marihuana. A lot of the young seem to think that's quite O.K., don't they? If not a public duty. But what they were carrying was heroin. Vast quantities of it, too, and this does seem to have shocked them. In fact, when you come to think of it, the poor saps were atrociously underpaid for the risks they ran.'

'Not the rate for the job?' Sophie inquired.

'Hardly. Anyway, having picked these two girls up, the police let Peregrine and Louise go on their way. They spent the night at a motel outside Southampton, on Monday made a round of their Hampshire pushers. Their contacts were arrested after they had left, and when they reached Willie's flat in the afternoon, all three of them were arrested. They still had quantities of heroin in the Citroën, too. And that's it. That's where we came in. The police are having a field day taking the flat apart, and the Chelsea studio, too, hoping to unearth a good deal about the racket in antiques as well as the drug network. Peregrine and Willie are going to spend a long time out of circulation, no doubt of it. We were lucky to get your sister into that clinic, you know. How has she settled down?'

'Badly.'

'I hope you made it clear to her that if it hadn't been for you're exertions – mine too, of course – she'd have been in Holloway instead?'

'I told her, yes.'

'But it didn't penetrate? No. I'm afraid you've got a problem there, all right.'

'He's noticed that for 'isself, Morry, you don't 'ave to tell 'im for 'im to know,' Leo pointed out. 'Now I suggest we stop mulling over past events – not to mention under-lining the obvious – and 'ave some nourish-ment instead, before we drop in our tracks.'

Morris Geldart retaliated instantly. His quiet professionalism disappeared, instead there was an inky schoolboy in the room, prodding Leo gleefully in his paunch. 'You great fat slob, you could live off that for months. I've got some work to do, if you haven't.' He and Leo left the room together, engaged, as far as could be seen, in trying to trip one another up. Before he left Geldart became serious again. 'See that lad of yours keeps in touch, won't you? He's had a tough time with his sister, I gather. Going to have a tougher, I'm afraid.'

This was what Nick was telling Sophie.

'We'll manage somehow,' Sophie reassured him. 'We'll look after her together.'

'Look, Sophie, you can't...'

'Last time you tried to cope on your own. Now at least you've got me. And Leo. And Morris Geldart.'

Full of confidence, he saw that she didn't understand what she would be letting herself in for, didn't grasp what it would be like. 'You'll stay out of it,' he said.

When Leo returned, Sophie immediately demanded his support. 'Nick's still maintaining I ought to stay away from him, never visit Minster Row. He seems to think Louise will be too much for me.'

'She's too much for me.'

'Much the best plan would be for us to get married, establish ourselves in your flat. Then at least we'll have a home to offer her. We'd be able to look after her more easily.'

'You can't live in Minster Row, to begin with.'

'Why not?'

'I don't think you can, you know,' Leo reinforced Nick.

'Why on earth not? If he can, I can. What's the difference?'

'I won't have it, and that's that.'

'I should wait until he's back at the Central, Soph,' Leo said cheerfully. 'It won't be long now. Only another couple of months, after all.'

Nick froze. Sophie turned a brilliant face towards Leo.

Unaffected, he continued. 'Because then

245

he can get a Central flat again. It's not worth moving in the meantime, I don't think.' He regarded them benignly. 'Well, I'm hungry, even if you aren't. We'll see what's in the frig.' He stumped off to the kitchen.

Sophie and Nick stared at each other. 'He must have meant it,' Sophie urged. 'He'd never have said it if he hadn't something planned.'

'I think he must mean it,' Nick agreed. Dazed, he followed Leo into the kitchen, found him peering inside the refrigerator, scrutinizing various little notes. 'Chicken curry,' he informed Nick. 'Half an hour at 350, rice in casserole, ditto, or smoked trout straight away.'

Nick paid no attention. 'Leo.' He'd never called him this before – at least not to his face – but neither of them noticed. 'What did you mean about being back at the Central in two months?'

'I make it about two months,' Leo confirmed, scouting about inside the refrigerator. 'There's steak, too.'

'Don't tease, Leo.' Sophie had joined them.

Leo came out of the frig, highly indignant. 'You're meant to be on my side, Soph.' He tweaked her long, honey-coloured hair. 'Not giving the game away like that. My secretary, aren't you?'

'Leo.' Nick ignored the chatter. '*What* job in two months?'

'My registrar, of course. That's when Johnnie finishes. You were supposed to be taking over from him, weren't you?'

'Yes, but...' Nick's voice died away, he leant against the sink.

'But what?' Leo sat down on the kitchen stool, regarded him. 'Don't you want it, then?' His dark eyes gleamed.

'Of course he does, Leo.' Sophie put an arm round Nick. 'He thought he'd said good-bye to the Central for ever, and now he's in a state of shock.' She stood on tiptoe, kissed Nick. 'Wake up, darling, and thank him properly. Oh, Leo, you are an *angel*.' Abandoning Nick, she flung her arms round Leo and kissed him on each cheek.

Leo hugged her, remarked, 'You kiss like a French general, Soph. But I must say it's very nice.'

'Leo, are you sure?' Nick had found his voice.

Leo grinned. 'I suppose you mean can I fix Steve King? If so, the answer is yes. I could've fixed 'im at the time, if you'd only 'ad the common to confide in me.'

'You weren't there.'

247

'If you'd 'ad the sense to tell Steve 'e'd 'ave understood, too. 'E might not 'ave liked it, 'e'd 'ave grumbled, but 'e'd 'ave backed you. 'E 'ad a lot of difficulty wiv 'is eldest. 'E got 'imself on drugs, up at Cambridge. L.S.D., that was. Nearly killed 'imself. You should 'ave told 'im, Nick.'

Nick flushed. 'I handled the whole affair in the worst possible way. I realize that now. But that's not the point. Look, are you sure you want me? I mean, I was supposed to have had two years' experience first, and – and I only had one, and made a mess of that, too. Since then I've simply been fiddling about in Cas. at Eversholt's. Are you sure I know enough to hold the job down adequately? I don't want to be a nuisance to you.'

'You won't be. The casualty experience isn't negligible, after all. And I shall start chasing you in me well known style. Now we'll 'ave supper, instead of standing about talking our 'eads off. We'd better 'ave the trout while we're waiting for the curry. I'm starving, even if you and Soph can feed on the love-light in y'r eyes.'

Nick had no notion, Leo brooded quietly to himself, how valuable he was going to be. Just as he'd said, he was short on experience still. But Stephen King had been freely admitting for months past that he'd made a mistake when he'd let him go. Even when unreliable, he'd said, Waring was twice as useful as Giles Stanstead. Giles was inclined to jump to conclusions, and too often to the wrong ones. Of course, the patients liked him, because he radiated confidence. They trusted him. Stephen King, though, didn't. He couldn't afford to.

What both Leo and Stephen King recognized was that Nick had the makings of one of the finest surgeons the Central had produced. There hadn't, after all, been that many. One or two in a generation only. Old Mummery himself, for instance, and Sandy Drummond. Both retired now. Northiam, the Central's present heart surgeon and an international figure. Perhaps Adam Trowbridge, who had succeeded Sandy Drummond in the orthopaedic department. Tom Rennison, whom they'd lost to Queen Alexandra's. Finally, when he was nearing retirement, Mummery had trained Leo, who knew that he owed everything to the old man, who alone had seen in a fat barrow boy from the back streets a surgeon the equal of any.

From his own experience, Leo understood

exactly how Nick felt. Until recently, Leo had never supposed his own surgical ability to be anything out of the ordinary run. Now, though, looking back over fifteen years, he could recognize that as a junior he must have shown exceptional promise. Without Mummery he would have been nowhere. Mummery had not only taught him all he knew, bullied him, borne with him, suffered from him. He'd fought for him, too. And Leo was well aware that he had not been the easiest of juniors to handle.

Now, in his turn, he would hand it all on. To Nick Waring. And he'd fight for Nick, too, as Mummery had fought for him.

He had no suspicion, though, how soon he was going to have to fight. For only two days later, in the middle of the afternoon, Nick had a call from the Berkshire clinic.

Louise was missing.

CHAPTER FOURTEEN

ON CALL

Nick put the telephone down, swore horribly. Sister Bowmaker, who had never seen him in such a mood, was astonished. ''Oo would ever 'ave thought it?' she confided to the switchboard. 'That nice quiet Dr Waring. The language 'e used after 'e'd 'ad that call. More like Tich when 'e's bin on the booze up at the market.'

Nick rang Morris Geldart. 'The clinic have telephoned. Louise was missing at lunch. Since then they've searched the house and grounds. No sign of her.'

Geldart sighed. 'Oh dear, what a pity,' he said mildly. 'If she doesn't turn up inside twenty-four hours I'll have to inform the court she's broken the terms of her bail.'

Nick rang Sophie at the Central. Leo, who happened to be in the office, demanded to know what had occurred.

Sophie explained.

'Tell 'im to come round this evening,' he

251

said. 'And we can talk it over. By then, of course, that ruddy sister of 'is may 'ave surfaced. I shouldn't be surprised if she didn't make straight for 'im. Where else can she go? So tell 'im that in that case, 'e can bring 'er along wiv 'im. I wanna 'ave a dekko at 'er, any'ow. Form my own opinion.'

Leo's forecast, as so often, proved correct. At seven o'clock that evening, Louise rang the bell in Minster Row. 'Only me,' she said, when he answered it, pushed quickly past him into the living room. 'I'm sorry I look so awful.' She was wearing old jeans and a dirty sweater, and her hair was dank and straggling. 'I simply had to get away from that place, though. You do understand that, don't you?'

'No,' he said shortly.

'Oh, but Nickie, if you knew what it was like…'

'Do you realize you've broken the law?'

'Oh, the law,' she said vaguely.

Useless to argue with her, he knew. 'I was just going over to Leo's. You can come with me.'

'Oh, but Nickie, I'm not dressed for going out anywhere. All my clothes are in that dreadful place still. Anyway, I don't want to go out, meet your draggy friends. All I want, what I came for, in fact, and you know perfectly well I simply must have it, and I thought that this time at least you'd understand and give me some. Please, Nickie, *please*. That's why I came.'

He understood only too well what she was asking for.

'Oh Nickie, please. I've got to have it, can't you see I must?'

He could. 'We'll go over to Leo's,' he said firmly. 'Once we're there I'll give Paul a ring, he'll probably come over and give you a shot. Tidy yourself up a bit, while I ring for a taxi.'

To his surprise she obeyed him, drifted off in the direction of the bathroom. He dialled the rank at King's Cross, was holding on for them when she came back into the room. 'If you won't give me a fix, Nickie,' she began, 'you can at least let me have some money. Then I can go out and buy what I need. I've taken everything I've got, but it's not nearly enough.'

He glanced up, the telephone in his hand. 'What have you taken?'

'Mind your own beeswax,' she said childishly. 'Give me some *cash*, Nickie, *Now.*'

'Don't be ridiculous, Lulu.'

'Ridiculous? It's my money as much as

yours, after all.'

This was a new theme. Or new to him, at least. No doubt this was what she had been handing out to Peregrine and Willie for months. Her next words bore this out.

'Willie says it shouldn't have gone to you. You're illegitimate, after all, aren't you? So that makes me the eldest. Because my parents were married.'

The glee in her voice startled him. He looked at her sharply. She was in a very bad state. Had she taken some toxic mixture of drugs? If so, he'd need help with her. He returned to the telephone, abandoned the taxi rank, which was still not answering, searched for the number of the treatment centre instead. He'd ask Paul to come over, if he was there. If not, anyone on duty.

'I want my money,' Louise was repeating. 'Money, Nickie. *Money*. That's what I came for.' She brought her hand from behind her. It held the carving knife from the kitchen.

Nick regarded it with extreme irritation.

'For heaven's sake, Lulu, stop playing the fool.'

'I'm not playing the fool. I mean it.'

'Oh, don't be so idiotic.'

'Idiotic? I'm simply asking for my own money. That I have a right to.'

254

He was unable to take this nonsense seriously. 'Look, love, calm down. There isn't any money here, for one thing, and for another...'

'Oh, isn't there? That's what you say, but you're lying, as usual. Everyone lies to me, but you're worse than the rest. You've done it all my life.'

Undoubtedly he needed Paul. He found the number, dialled.

But too late.

'Put that telephone down. You're only going to talk about me on it. And I won't have people talking about me. Put it *down*.'

He looked up at her. The line was ringing in the treatment centre.

Louise lunged forward, pressed her finger down, cut him off. 'See?' she said triumphantly. 'I'm the one who decides, Nickie. From now on. Not you. I've had enough of being ordered about, told what to do and where to go. Now it's going to be you who does what I say.'

They stared at one another like a couple of boxers.

'Stand up,' Louise said. She brandished the knife in front of his nose.

'Stop waving that thing about,' he said crossly.

'Stand up, Nickie, or I'll cut you with it.'

He stood up.

'Turn out your pockets.'

He began feeling in them.

'Quickly.' She prodded him with the tip of the knife, giggled. She was delighted with herself, and high as they come. He had to act, and fast.

He produced his wallet, held it momentarily in front of her, dropped it on the sofa.

As he had foreseen, she stretched for it avidly. He reached for her at the same moment, grabbed both her wrists.

Louise screamed, twisted and turned. She was uncontrollable, no longer responsible for her actions. She could do anything, he knew.

And at that moment she did.

As they stood jostling and wrestling, Nick exerted his strength and bent her wrist, forced her to drop the knife. But she caught it with her other hand as it fell, made a wild swipe across his wrist.

Blood spurted up in their faces, hit the ceiling, gushed like a water spout. A red water spout.

Both of them sprang back, shocked into silence. Nick automatically put his own right hand over the bleeding artery, while his mind raced.

He had two or three minutes to ensure his survival. No more. After that he'd lose consciousness, bleed to death inside ten minutes.

Louise was as shocked as he was. She was not as far gone as he'd feared. She dropped the knife, stared. 'Oh, Nickie.' It was a whisper only. 'Oh Nickie darling, I am so *sorry.*' She wiped her hand over her face, wet with his blood, gazed at it blankly. *'Nickie.'* It was a child's wail for comfort.

But he had no time for comfort. He couldn't trust her to remain like this. He let go of his wrist, saw his own blood shoot towards the ceiling again. Summoning all his reserves, he hit her hard. To his relief the strong left hook to the jaw that Mathew had taught him as a boy knocked her out. She crumpled immediately. He could only hope she'd stay out until help came. Holding on to his wrist again, he sat down on the floor, reached for the telephone. Useless to attempt to ring Eversholt's. Ironically, the only man there geared to deal with an emergency like this was himself. Even the switchboard would have been taken over by one of the Spanish porters. And while Eversholt's had no colour problem, its mixed races co-existing cheerfully, it did have language barriers. English was used as a working language, of course, but the Indian registrars often failed to understand the English spoken by the Spanish, while the African, West Indian or Malaysian nurses could barely comprehend one another, let alone get across to the Indians or the Spanish. Nick doubted if he'd ever be able to convey to the Spaniard his need for treatment. He shook his head. He could die waiting on Eversholt's switchboard.

Sister Bowmaker upstairs? But he had no breath to shout, even if he'd had any hope of making himself heard above the television and the traffic noise. Ridiculously, he had no idea what her telephone number was. He'd never needed it. No time to hunt for it now, even if he'd still been capable of walking across the room to fetch the directory.

He'd known all along what he was going to do, and his busy fingers were already dialing the familiar number. Leo. He'd act faster than anyone. There'd be no delay, no failure in communication. In Leo's hands he'd be safe. Louise too.

Leo, lying back in his Charles Eames chair, feet up on the black leather stool, chatting lazily to Sophie about the day's patients, raised an eyebrow as the telephone shrilled and remarked. 'Ere we go again. 'Oo is it going to be now?' He stretched out a hand for the instrument, announced 'Rosenstein.'

His feet hit the floor, the chair swivelled on its base, swung. 'I'll be over *stat.*' Even as he spoke one hand was reaching for his bag. The other clattered the telephone back and he was at the door. 'Come with me, Soph. Tell you in the lift what I want. Leave the door open. You'll be back.'

He leant on the lift bell. 'That was Nick. Radial artery slashed, 'e said.'

The lift arrived. Leo crashed the gates back, stepped in. 'Come on.' He crashed the gates again, pressed the ground floor button.

'Get 'old of Johnnie – or anyone else you can if 'e's not available. Send 'im over to give me an 'and. Radial artery haemorrhage, tell 'im. 'E'll know what to bring.'

They reached the ground, Leo raced out of the lift. Sophie, pale, shaking, closed the doors, returned upwards to the flat. She went straight to the telephone, began to dial the familiar Central number.

Then she remembered. Sister Bowmaker. Upstairs, in Minster Row.

For a split second Sophie panicked. This

was contrary to Leo's instructions. And was she justified in spending valuable seconds hunting for a number?

But if Sister Bowmaker was at home, she'd be down with Nick before Leo could reach him.

Her fingers were ruffling through the pages of the directory. Here it was. Damn, two numbers. Must be shop and home. This looked like home. Try it first, anyway. The telephone was answered almost at once. Against a background of what sounded like a combined day nursery and building site, came a confident voice Sophie recognized.

When Leo screeched to a halt and hurled himself down the area steps, the basement door was opened for him immediately by Tich Bowmaker. 'Through here,' he said.

Apart from the blood, which was everywhere, the first sight to meet Leo's eyes was a pair of feet pointing skywards and attached to legs resting against the arm of the sofa. Propping them there, and with Nick's left wrist nearly as high, enclosed in her capable grip, was a buxom figure attired in bedroom slippers, trousers, a fair-isle sweater with the sleeves pushed up, hair in rollers – Sister Bowmaker in evening dress.

'Mr Rosenstein?' she greeted him, as poised as if she'd been in charge of her own department. 'Your secretary rang,' she added. 'Sister Bowmaker, from Eversholt's.'

Leo mentally took off his hat to Sophie. It was not often he overlooked a point, but on the occasions when he did, she could be relied on.

''Ow is 'e?'

''E's lost consciousness. But 'e'd strapped 'is wrist with 'is tie, and in fact 'e was still 'olding on to it when I got 'ere, so I don't think 'e need 'ave lost all that blood. Apart from right at the beginning, that is.' Her expert eye traversed floor and ceiling, years of experience behind her assessment, she said, 'Over three pints, though, I'd say.'

'Think so? Enough blood about to float an armada. I suppose that's that damned sister of 'is down there?'

Both Bowmakers shook their heads. They couldn't say.

''Ooever she is, she's out for the count,' Tich volunteered. 'Reckon she went for 'im with the knife, and 'e landed 'er one.' He shoved the knife with his toe.

'Take it away,' Leo said. 'She might come round.' He was taking Nick's pulse with one hand, opening his bag with the other.

'Tich. 'Elp Mr Rosenstein with 'is bag.'

'Can still get his pulse, anyway. What I think we'd better do first, sister, is clamp the artery. So if you'd...'

They worked together.

Five minutes later Sophie and Johnnie arrived with plasma and oxygen.

''E's alive, Soph.' Leo said. 'Sister saw to that. Sensible of you to get on to 'er. Probably saved Nick's life, that did. But now it's the next few hours that are going to be crucial. We must get some plasma in, restore 'is circulation.'

Sophie's eyes travelled round the blood-spattered room, came back to rest on Nick.

'You could make up the fire,' Leo spared a glance for her. 'We want the room as warm as possible. And get blankets.'

Half an hour later, his face hidden by the oxygen mask, a bottle of plasma emptying itself into one arm, his wrist bandaged and splinted, Nick was swathed in blankets. Johnnie was taking his blood pressure. His colour was bad still, and he was very cold. Almost on his shoulders on the floor, his feet and legs were upended against the sofa, as they had been all along – he'd put them there himself, before he passed out.

Tich Bowmaker had gone to the Central

'Used to it. Doesn't often show nowadays.' He grinned amiably, apparently in an excellent humour. 'Eat up,' he urged her.

After a mushroom omelette, a pot of coffee, innumerable slices of toast and marmalade, Leo was ready for a day's work. 'You 'ave a good kip this morning,' he said. 'Come in this afternoon, eh?'

Sophie had her own ideas about this. All she said was, 'I'd like to have a look at Nick.'

'We'll both go and see 'im.'

He was heavily sedated, barely conscious. Even so, his face could still light up for Sophie. She searched for his hand, but one arm was extended in splints and bandages to prevent movement from disturbing the still vulnerable artery, while the other was in use for a drip. So she laid her fingers momentarily against his cheek, smiled back at him. He murmured something she was unable to catch, and she leant forward.

'Lulu?' he was asking. 'Is she all right? I hit her,' he added.

'Paul Worsley came round and saw to her,' Sophie explained. 'He took her to the treatment centre. She's very upset, he says, and needs psychiatric care. He'll transfer her to St Botolph's. He told me to tell you he thought the court would probably accept the move as a necessary transfer for treatment. So I'll ring Morris Geldart this morning and explain what's happened. Paul says he'll back me up.'

Nick muttered again.

Sophie couldn't get the faint whisper, had to ask him to repeat it.

'Is she all right otherwise?'

'Paul seems to think so,' Sophie considered this a moderate and restrained reply on her part. All right, indeed, she seethed inwardly. While Nick might easily have died.

'She didn't mean it,' he pointed out. Astonishingly, blue eyes danced, while the wide mouth curved into laughter. 'I love you when you look furious like that.'

Sophie simmered.

'Of course, I love you anyway,' he added, watching her still. 'Don't go away, will you?'

'She's going away now, Nick,' Leo said from the end of the bed. 'She can come back and sit with you for a bit this afternoon.'

Neither of them attempted to argue with him.

When Sophie returned, Nick lay, like a personality from show business, in a bower of flowers. Spring had come, and the Bowmakers had brought it to the Central, transferring half the contents of their shop to his room. Daffodils and narcissus filled the air with perfume, freesia too, while pots of hyacinths, blue, white and pink, added their scent to the heady atmosphere. Jonquils and early tulips stood in vases, a big shallow bowl held massed bunches of snowdrops. Gilt baskets sporting huge bows were bursting with oranges and apples, grapes, bananas and pears. Dotted about was an assortment of get well cards of the more vulgar type – on sale at the newsagents opposite Eversholt's – from almost everyone at the hospital, where Sister Bowmaker and the switchboard had spread a lurid account of the night's events with supersonic speed.

'Tich came in his van,' Nick explained. 'There are more in the ward,' he added apologetically.

Sophie picked her way cautiously through the floral tributes. The flowers disconcerted her – she had come prepared to do battle. 'I'm going to insist that we get married before he even thinks of going back to that flat,' she had told Leo belligerently.

He'd eyed her. 'It's not me you have to convince. I'm with you all the way. I like to see my staff nicely settled. And you can't do better. Nor can young Nick. Tell you another thing, 'e needs you to make 'im start thinking about 'imself occasionally. I'm tired of seeing someone with all 'e 'as to offer consistently putting 'imself at risk. If 'e'd bin brought up in the back streets, like me, 'e'd know 'ow to look after No.1.'

'Oh yes? That's what made you go in for medicine, I suppose? Not to mention stay up night after night looking after the sick and injured?'

'Me Dad thought it would be nice to 'ave a doctor in the family, see? And I got a scholarship. And I expect 'e thought wiv any luck I'd be able to keep 'im in 'is old age, too.'

'And will you?'

Leo's eyes glinted. 'Me old man 'as made 'is pile since then. Like I said, 'e knows 'ow to look after 'imself. But young Nick don't. So you'd better do it for 'im.'

'He loves Louise, you know.'

'More than she deserves. 'Owever, I'll admit that that's one of the advantages of love. It don't 'ave to be deserved. 'E's got a lot of love to offer, of course. More than most. And you'll always be able to rely on 'im. She can, we've all seen that, and you can expect all 'e gives 'er, and more. Because 'e loves you more.'

'And I love him,' Sophie said softly.

'So you go right a'ead and take 'im over, ducks. I was against you living in that slum at one time, I know, but you'll be okay there for a month or two. You'll have Sister Bowmaker upstairs, any'ow. What more can you ask?'

'I don't ask any more,' Sophie had said. And now here she was, with her arguments rehearsed. But the flowers, and the sight of Nick still so tired and pale, made her forget her lines. She could get nothing out.

Her arms went round him, though, and suddenly he was saying it all for her. 'All I could think was what a bloody stupid waste,' he said. 'I was going to die without us ever having been together for more than a few snatched hours.' He smiled unexpectedly. 'At least it made me determined to fight like hell to stay alive. So here I am. And here you are. We'll get married, shall we, as soon as I can walk out of this place? Tomorrow, say? Not really fair to you, of course, but we'll manage.'

'Yes,' Sophie said. It turned out to be all that needed saying.

This Large Print Book, for people
who cannot read normal print,
is published under the auspices of

THE ULVERSCROFT FOUNDATION